ABBY'S
Pony Love

When a girl falls in pony-love,
she wants it to be forever.

Publisher's Cataloging-in-Publication Data

Names: Count, Susan, author. | Johnson, Bev, illustrator.
Title: Abby's pony love / Susan Count, illustrated by Bev Johnson.
Description: Huntsville, TX : Hastings Creations Group, 2022. | Includes b&w illustrations and diagrams. | Series: Dream pony riders ; 1. | Audience: Ages 8-12. | Summary: At her stable job, Abby falls in love with a beautiful but mischievous pony, only to have it bought by another family. Her heart aches when her job becomes helping the new owner learn to ride the best pony ever. Can she let go of what never belonged to her?
Identifiers: LCCN 2021906952 | ISBN 9781952371042 (hardcover) | ISBN 9781952371035 (pbk.) | ISBN 9781952371028 (ebook)
Subjects: LCSH: Ponies — Juvenile fiction. | Emotions — Juvenile fiction. | Perseverance (Ethics) — Juvenile fiction. | Friendship — Juvenile fiction. | Stables — Juvenile fiction. | BISAC: JUVENILE FICTION / Animals / Horses. | JUVENILE FICTION / Social Themes / Friendship. | JUVENILE FICTION / Sports & Recreation / Equestrian.
Classification: LCC PZ7.1 C68 A23 2022 | DDC [Fic]—dc22
LC record available at https://lccn.loc.gov/2021906952

DEDICATION

Glory to God. May the works of my hands bring honor to the house of the Lord.

DREAM PONY RIDERS BOOK 1

ABBY'S

SUSAN COUNT

TABLE OF CONTENTS

CHAPTER ONE

BARN JOB

A horse drawing taped to the frozen yogurt shop door fluttered.

"Horseback Riding Lessons? Dream Horse Stables." Even though riding lessons were impossible, Abby couldn't look away. Then tiny print across the bottom of the flyer drew her closer. "Working student position available."

I can work. Perfect! I need to get this job.

As she hurried home, she strategized how to ask her parents. She wouldn't chicken out. This was her big break to be near horses. Might be her only chance since they'd made it clear they were never going to buy her one.

Even as her hands trembled, she took extra care setting the table. She adjusted the spacing between the fork and the plate ever so precisely, then arranged a white cloth napkin. If she served it up right, they might let her apply for the barn job. "Wash your hands for dinner," she told her sisters as Dad set food on the table.

Mom entered the house in slow motion, kicked her black pumps under a chair, and placed each thing she carried onto it, barely making a sound. She turned the cell phone ringer off and sighed as she settled at the dinner table. Closing her eyes, she seemed to concentrate on her breathing. Maybe this wasn't the best time.

Abby set the rooster salt and pepper shakers right by Dad's place. As she sat, she caught his eye. "This roast smells fantastic."

"Thanks, brown eyes. I had it in the oven on low all afternoon." Dad dolloped mashed potatoes next to the roast on his plate. "I'm becoming quite a good cook if I do say so myself."

"Since you make amazing gravy, you can take over that job permanently." Mom grinned. "Right, girls?"

The twins and Abby all giggled like they were in on a grand conspiracy.

When the laughter quieted, Abby took her best shot. "Speaking of jobs." She swallowed hard, wiping her nervous sweat on her yellow stretch pants. "There's a flyer on the door of the frozen yogurt store about a barn job at that equestrian center by the park. A working student position. If I can get the job, they'd give me horseback riding lessons in exchange for barn chores."

Dad reached for the butter. "Since school's going to start in just over a month, isn't it too late to add such a time-consuming activity?"

"But I'm a great student. I almost got all A's last quarter. I can handle it. I promise."

"Sounds fun, but I'm sorry." Mom shook her head. "I need you to take care of the twins."

"But they're going to be ten next month," Abby objected. "Can't they stay out of trouble until Tara gets home?" She withered under her mom's steady gaze and clamped her teeth together to keep her tongue from wagging. Had she gone too far?

Mom sighed. "You know the answer."

Just like that, the family's good cheer and Abby's hopes flushed away. Her older sister, Tara, had been responsible for the twins until she got the job at the discount store. Now she worked long hours trying to save college money, and the babysitting responsibilities passed to Abby.

The twins looked at each other and said in unison, "We're old enough."

"I don't think so." Mom set her fork down. "You girls are way too young to be left alone."

Dad pulled a roll from the breadbasket. "I agree, but I—"

"I get it," Abby interrupted. "It's my turn to babysit, so I can't do what sounds like the best job ever."

"Go to your room, young lady." The sudden stern in Dad's

voice said Abby'd crossed the line. "Think about how rude you're being."

"Don't come out until you are ready to apologize," Mom added.

"Yes, ma'am," Abby answered politely, but in her mind, she shoved back her chair and stormed to her room.

She sat at her desk and drummed quietly with her fists. "This is not fair." She ranted to the girl in the mirror. "So what are you going to do about it?"

She crossed her arms as she waited for an answer. "You going to give up and hide behind a book like you always do? This is your only shot. You've got to go for it."

Reason calmed her anger. *Five minutes to six o'clock. I'm running out of day. I've got to fix this fast.*

She opened her decorated box of inspirational quotes and flipped through the colored note cards. "There's got to be something in here that will help."

A yellow card poked up and she pinched it from the others.

" 'When all your eyes see is darkness, look for the light with your heart.' " She tossed the card on the desk and picked up another. " 'When all hope is gone, pray for a miracle.' "

Hmm, miracles are good.

" 'If things aren't going as planned, it's because God has a better plan.' "

She dropped the cards back into the box. "That's what I need—a better plan."

She stood. With a deep breath, she faced her failures. To the mirror, she said, "Be sorry. Be sincere. Beg."

When Abby returned to the kitchen, Mom worked on her computer. Dad chunked a detergent pod into the dishwasher and shut the door.

He sat at the table with Mom. "That was fast."

"I'm so sorry. I was horrible and rude."

"And?"

"It won't happen again." Abby hung her head.

"See that it doesn't."

She nodded that she understood. "I know it's up to me and I love the twins, but I've never wanted anything so much. I've always loved horses. I'm really sorry."

Mom stilled her fingers over the keyboard and gave Abby a stern look she knew well. "Frankly, we were leaning toward grounding you for the rest of the summer, but your outburst is uncharacteristic of you."

"Your mom and I want to give you credit—you're a great student. That doesn't happen without a lot of hard work and commitment."

"I try hard. But I'm not good at making friends. I could make friends with a horse or other girls like me who love horses."

"You bring up an interesting point. Friendships tend to be formed around a common interest." Dad leaned on his elbows. "Before you erupted into a girl we didn't recognize, I was about to say I could take responsibility for the twins when you're at the barn."

Abby's lips parted, and soon, her mouth gaped open.

"Your mom and I talked about this situation while we

cleaned up after dinner. I believe we can agree the apology sounded sincere." Dad paused as if rethinking his conclusion. "If you think you can handle such a big commitment then, until I find another job, I'll deal with the twins. It would be good for you. And, like you point out, it would bring you in contact with other girls who love what you love."

The barn doors to Abby's dream flew open. She hugged her parents with all the joy she felt. One hurdle leaped. One to go. "Can I go ask about the job? The barn manager might need someone on the weekends. I could for sure do that? Right?"

"Now?" Mom glanced at the clock and frowned. "You've hardly touched your dinner. And what about your summer literature class?"

"I finished the report for my required reading, and I'm almost done with the extra credit book. It's about a girl in a wheelchair and a foal born with a clubfoot. Then she finds out the foal will be put to sleep. You just know she has to save the foal, but it looks hopeless. It's so exciting. I can't wait to finish it." Abby rushed her words to not give Mom an opening to stop her. "I've got to go now. If I wait, someone else might get the job. It has to be now. It's early yet. There's always someone at a barn."

Mom raised her hand. "Go then. I agree with Dad. Plus, exercise would be good for you."

"Come on." Dad motioned for her to follow him to the garage. "I'll help you with your bike." He handed her the air pump. She filled the tires while he tightened the nut holding the handlebars. "There ya go."

"Thanks." She pushed off and coasted down the driveway, her golden brown hair streaming behind her. As she pedaled, she rehearsed her speech. "Hi. I'm Abby. I'm twelve and in the seventh grade. I love horses, and I'm a good student and a hard worker. I know a lot about horses because I've read books about them in the school library. I saw your flyer, and I'd like to apply for the working student position. I can start now." *Not bad.*

The stable was only ten minutes away on her bike. She'd ridden by once and watched the girls jumping—such beautiful ponies. But she'd been too shy to talk to anyone. Would she get there to apply for the job only to chicken out? What if they already gave the job to someone else?

She propped the crummy bike on its kickstand. It held. As soon as she turned her back, the bike toppled onto the blacktop. She picked it up and settled it against a shrub. "You're better than nothin', but not by much."

She paused to take in the barn's beauty. A red softened with age coated its outside. The long alley lured her into the barn. Birds chirped and flitted through the cobweb-covered rafters. One horse whinnied and another answered. The stalls were small boxes with wooden doors. The hinges must be the originals. The latches looked like rusty prayers to keep in the horses. Each stall had a blue hook to hold a halter. A wheelbarrow angled to the side as if someone left off doing a disagreeable chore. The strong smell as she passed the wheelbarrow made her nose run. But what overwhelmed her were the faces looking at her as she stepped into the shaded barn. Horses and ponies of all sizes and colors.

"Wow," she breathed, wanting to touch each one. An Appaloosa pony thrust his head over the stall door, and his nose demanded her attention. "Later, I can fall in love with you later. First, I need to get the job."

With a surge of determination, she pulled her shoulders back and strode through the barn looking for the office. A musical voice traveled toward her. Drawing near to a room with a light on, Abby waited in the doorway for the young woman to finish her phone call.

Dressed in breeches and a long-sleeved blouse, the woman tilted her head and nodded along with the speaker. "Yes, ma'am. I'll make sure to take care of it."

When the woman hung up and saw Abby, surprise registered on her pretty face. "Can I help you?"

Sweat dripped from Abby's underarms and soaked the inside of her arms. She shifted and gnawed on her upper lip. *What am I doing here? I know nothing.*

"I'm Elena. I'm the barn manager and the head trainer. Are you here about horseback riding lessons?"

Abby stared at the trainer. Her tongue tied in knots, and she couldn't make it work.

"I'm a certified instructor. I grew up and trained in classical dressage in Andalusia, Spain. That's the Andalusian horse capital of the world. I've been teaching here for three years. I'll have you riding confidently in no time."

It must have been obvious Abby forgot the question because the trainer repeated it. "You're here to take lessons, right? We have classes starting up this week."

Abby nodded yes. Then she shook her head no. Not one word of her speech could she remember. "Work—working student?"

"Ah, yes. Come in." Miss Elena lifted a pile of folded horse blankets from a chair and motioned for her to sit. "What experience do you have?"

"Experience?" *Could she say* none *out loud? How does someone get experience anyway?* "I—I've read a lot. I love horses."

"I see. While I expected to train the right person, I need someone experienced. Would you like to sign up for lessons?"

"I'm a good student, and I learn fast."

At a loss for words, the barn manager looked away and cleared her throat. Abby filled the gap. "I—I'm a hard worker, and nobody would try harder than me."

"I appreciate that, but you're not what I had in mind. I'm sorry."

Abby lowered her chin to her chest. She muttered, "Thank you, anyway." Determined not to cry, she focused on her feet and forced them to walk away.

Behind her, the manager rattled in a closet. Then quick sweeps of a broom patted the concrete floor.

Abby turned to watch. She walked to the closet like she owned it and pulled out another broom. Following a few steps to the rear of the young woman, Abby mimicked her sweeping action.

At the end of the aisle, the woman reversed. "I thought you left."

"There's work to do, and I need experience." Abby swept to the end of the concrete. Gripping the broom handle, she locked her eyes onto the manager's face. *Look confident. Isn't that what Dad said about job interviews?* "I'd be a big help. I'm strong. I just want to hang out around horses. Nothing smells like they do. The sounds they make in the barn make me smile. Their feet shuffling in the bedding. The grinding noise when they eat hay. They are amazing."

The barn manager studied her.

Abby squirmed under the woman's steady gaze.

"My worker quit right before my training classes are scheduled to start. All this at the same time is too much for me." Miss Elena gestured toward the stalls. "I need serious experienced help here."

"Since you don't have anyone else right now, could you give me a trial? I'll work for free. You won't even have to give me lessons. I'm dependable and responsible."

As the manager gave a barely perceptible shake of her head, Abby gathered her courage and pitched her last shot. "Did someone give you a chance once?"

Miss Elena rubbed her neck. "Someone *did* give me a chance once. I wouldn't be here without her having believed in me. And I am a bit desperate."

The trainer's deep sigh gave Abby hope. "I'll give you a trial."

"You won't be sorry. You'll see."

"Your enthusiasm counts for a lot. My schedule is all messed up today. It's time to feed." Miss Elena gestured to the horses looking at her. "I'll show you the routine. Follow me." She opened the feed room door across from the office. "Toss a couple bales of hay onto that cart."

Abby jumped to the haystacks. When she tugged on the strings, the bale barely moved.

"You'll need to throw muscle into it. They weigh about fifty-five pounds. We toss hay first. It helps keep them quiet while we get the grain out." Miss Elena demonstrated as she talked. "Pull this lever, and it fills the can with feed. It's on wheels, but it's heavy." She drew Abby into the aisle. "Each horse has two water buckets hanging in their stall, and they have to be refilled at every feeding."

"Got it."

"Always notice what they've eaten. If they turn away from food or if they left food in the feed bucket or if the water's not been touched, I need to know—immediately. A quick response can mean the difference between a horse surviving an illness—or not."

Abby forced a swallow. She'd pushed her way into this job. But was she up to the responsibility? Could she do this job when she knew nothing about horses except what she'd read in books?

"Each stall has a whiteboard on it with the horse's name and what it gets fed. Pay close attention. A change in diet can cause a horse to colic."

She gulped. When her fear remained stuck in her throat, she gulped again. Would the manager notice?

Miss Elena rapped on a whiteboard nailed to the wall

over the feed bins. "This is the health tracking chart for each animal in my care. I record their annual shots, teeth floats, worming, and farrier schedule here. If an owner comes into the barn and asks you questions, this is where you come. Say as little as possible because, if they sense you don't know what you're doing, they will draw blood—yours. Understand?"

Abby nodded like she understood. *Floats? Worms? Blood?*

"Any questions?" When Abby shook her head, the manager continued, "It'll be your responsibility to be here for the afternoon feedings starting tomorrow. If you're still here once school starts, you can pick up extra hours on Saturdays or anytime you have a day off."

"I'll still be here!" Abby declared with great confidence. "Thank you so much. You won't be sorry." She spun and waved her arms. "I'll be the best helper you've ever had."

"Let's see how it goes. Consider the next two weeks a trial period, so show me what you can do." Miss Elena added a quick note to the board and turned back to her. "You should know—if the horse owners don't like the job you're doing, you're out."

The cold truth returned the serious to Abby's demeanor. "Of course. I'll make them very happy."

Abby practically skipped down the barn aisle. She wanted to leap and click her heels together. The Appaloosa pony that greeted her on the way in left his hay manger and hung his head over his stall's half door, watching her.

"You again." She stopped to rub him. "Sorry, I don't have any treats. I won't let it happen again. Aren't you handsome?"

The pony tilted his head to the side and flapped his lips as she scratched his withers.

Abby read the sign on his stall. "Your name is Freckles? With all those spots, that name suits you. So what's your story? Do you belong to some lucky girl who loves you over the moon?"

She drew her hand back, and Freckles flipped his nose. "You weren't done with me yet? I can't stay all night, you know." She gave him another rub. "You're so sweet. I wish I could have a pony of my own. Just like sweet-and-sour candy, you make me happy, then sad. I'll be back tomorrow to feed you. And the day after that and the day after that. If your owner likes me anyway."

CHAPTER TWO

LEARN THE ROPES

Three days later, Abby hummed as she swept the tack room. A young woman, dressed to ride, glared at her and pulled a saddle from the rack.

"You the new girl?" The woman's tone jolted Abby.

"Yes, ma'am. I'm Abby."

The woman shook out a white pad and laid it across the saddle. "New or not, you better not ever skip filling my horse's water buckets again. I came back to the barn yesterday to check on him after our jumping lesson. I'm so glad I did. Both buckets only had an inch of water." She started to the door. "My horse is Black Jack. Make sure you take good care of him, or I'll have to speak to Elena."

"I'm sure I filled all the buckets." Biting her lip, Abby pondered filling the buckets. "But I'll double-check from now on."

"See that you do."

"Yes, ma'am." She continued sweeping, but she worried the whole time she did the barn chores. After she mucked out a stall, she inspected her work before she moved to the next stall. Once she filled the water buckets, she breezed from stall to stall double-checking. *I have to do this right and keep Miss Elena happy.*

As Abby loaded two bales of hay onto the rolling cart, a tall, thin woman stepped into the feed room. "I heard there was a new girl."

"I'm Abby." *Now, what did I do?*

"Well, Abby, we will get along just fine if you make sure my horse gets the right amount of hay every night. He only had one flake in his rack last night, and it clearly says he gets two." She tapped on her horse's name on the board. "Top Hand. Two flakes. Got it?"

"Yes, ma'am." *I can't please anybody.*

Abby shut the feed room door and secured the second latch, taking no chances any of the horses could get in. She'd already gotten a humiliating lecture from a girl younger than her about how a horse would eat everything in the feed room and die. The girl's name was Lily. She looked delicate like a flower, but when it came to her pony, she was tough like a weed.

A woman dressed in tan breeches walked a tall bay horse past Abby. When she smiled, Abby smiled back. *Finally someone nice.*

The woman stopped at the stall entrance. "Oh come on."

"Is something wrong?" *Here it comes.*

"I'm getting so tired of the lax way this barn is managed. Look at this."

Abby leaned into the stall. "What? I don't see anything."

"Has no one ever told you about cleaning out the bedding wet spots?"

"Um… yes." Suddenly, Abby needed to run to the bathroom in the worst way. "But I've only been here three days, and I don't see a wet spot."

"Get me a rake and the muck bucket, and I'll show you." The woman tied the gelding outside the stall as Abby did as she was told. The owner took the rake and walked to the stall's far side. She skimmed the dry surface bedding away, revealing a soggy, packed mass. As the ammonia smell assaulted her nose, Abby's disbelief changed to embarrassment. The woman scooped and deposited it in the cart. "You have to know the habits of the horses in your care." She handed the rake back to Abby, who finished the job.

I'm beginning to understand what Miss Elena meant about the owners leaving me bloody.

By the end of her first week, despite everything she learned the hard way, Abby was in love with every one of the horses. If only all she had to deal with were the horses, her new life at the barn would be perfect.

A pack of three girls sauntered into the alleyway laughing and joking.

"Hi. I'm Abby." She flashed her best smile. As she held her hand up in greeting, they bustled past as if she was nothing more than a hay bale. Their clothes were perfect, their hair was perfect, and their horses were perfect. Abby had to face reality—she was a regular tomboy. She popped into the nearest stall and whispered to the horse in it. "Can I hide out with you for a few minutes? Those girls think they are the divas of the horse world. I don't know—maybe they are. And I'm muck on their boots." She craned her neck to see if they were gone. "Thanks, buddy. I'll share my next apple with you."

She patted the horse, hurried out the front of the barn, and pedaled her bike home.

Saturday had always been Abby's favorite day of the week. Now it was a superstar day because both Mom and Dad were home with the twins, so she could stay at the barn as long as she wanted. Feeding horses early in the morning was the best job ever after she learned to avoid the owners. She loved walking in, having them recognize her, and lighting up the barn with nickers. She practiced an efficient rhythm to get each horse fed as fast as possible. The better she got, the happier and quieter the herd waited. 'Course, there was the grumpy one. Rio. Twelve hands and three inches high of tough guy. She'd tried feeding him first and feeding him last. It didn't matter which, he still bared his teeth at the mare next door and lunged at her like he was a pony devil. After the meal, he was a little lamb. Maybe she should mention it to Miss Elena. *It's probably just the way he is, and I'll look like I don't know anything—which I don't.*

The serious look on Miss Elena's face as she came toward Abby caused her to tense. *Did I do something? Not do something?*

"Busy day today. Did you see my instructions for you? They are by the list on the board with vet appointments."

Abby hated to admit she hadn't checked the board. Her blank look must have said it all.

"Give the horses on the list a flake of hay and turn the rest out to pasture. Then come talk to me. We need to chat."

Oh, that's bad. Miss Elena's exasperated sigh hurt. Couldn't she see how hard Abby was trying?

"Yes, ma'am." Abby checked the board. Five: Buttercup, Jingle, Tex, Fancy, Candy. Then she loaded the cart with a hay bale and moved along the aisle, feeding each one. *Someone complained, and I'm going to be fired.*

When she came to Rio, he grunted and kicked the stall wall. "You're not starving, and you're going out to pasture. How about I take you out first? That make you happy?" She slipped a handful of loose hay between the bars, and he quieted. The horse's behavior nagged at her. Maybe she should ask Miss Elena to look at Rio.

Abby waited in Miss Elena's office doorway while the manager ordered feed. She glanced around, reached into her shirt, and picked out hay pieces scratching her skin. Then the barn manager gestured for her to sit in the chair before the desk.

This is serious. I'm in big trouble here. Abby rubbed her fingers together like she was trying to start a fire. *I've been doing okay. Who complained? The Divas would love to get me in trouble.*

When Miss Elena finished, she closed the feed store binder and shuffled papers to the side before focusing on Abby's face. If only a trapdoor would open underneath her and whisk her away! Then Miss Elena smiled. "I want to talk to you about your job here."

If it weren't for the smile, Abby would have burst into tears.

"Most of the owners are quite happy with your work, and if they are pleased, I'm pleased. You'll never please all of them, but you've gone out of your way to be helpful and to learn the routines. I had serious doubts about your being able to do this job, but you have exceeded my expectations continually. Coming in—on your own—to help with the morning feeding demonstrated a work ethic I don't often see."

"Thank you." Abby warmed.

"I've been authorized to start paying you a small salary on top of the lessons."

"Oh, wow! That's great." She pumped her hands in the air. "I'm going to save to buy my own pony."

"I understand wanting your own, but there are advantages to riding other people's horses. Well then..." Miss Elena winked. "Get to work before you get in trouble with the boss."

Abby jumped up, then hesitated. She didn't dare say the wrong thing and sound like she knew nothing, even if it was the truth. But she had to take a chance because the horse might be sick or something. "Rio. It's about Rio."

"Ah. He's too much horse for your first lesson. I was planning to put you up on Freckles. He's my best beginner lesson horse."

"I'd love to ride Freckles, but...."

"Usually Saturday is my busiest lesson day." Miss Elena searched a file cabinet. "But this is the only day the vet could come this week, so I had to cancel morning lessons. I have time to get you started. How's that sound?"

"Great. Except...."

"No need to worry. We'll go slow."

"That's not it."

"What is it then?"

"I wonder if Rio feels bad. He's the grumpiest one in the barn at feed time. I didn't turn him out because I thought you'd want to check him."

Miss Elena passed around Abby and hurried to the gelding's stall. "How long have you noticed this behavior?"

"Two or three days."

"He needs to be checked. Could be an ulcer. I'll add him to the list for the vet." Miss Elena rested a hand on Abby's shoulder. "Good job noticing a change in him. It's so important to be observant. I use him for my intermediate lessons. If we put a rider up and he felt bad, he could act out and hurt one of our young equestrians."

Finally, she did something right! Abby could hardly wait for the vet to arrive. She watched for his truck and hovered near Rio. A dually white truck with a big steel box in the bed parked in front. *Has to be him.* She slipped Rio's halter on and put him first in line in the crossties.

Miss Elena smiled at her like she understood. "Put Candy next to Rio, and I'll bring Fancy."

Abby hurried to stand with Rio, rubbing his neck reassuringly. "Going to find out what bothers you and make it right."

The vet nodded as he listened to Abby describe her observations, but he watched Miss Elena the whole time. It only took him a few minutes to check the animal.

"I don't find anything obvious." He turned back to Miss Elena. "Has he shown any signs of being colicky?"

"None. And he's doesn't react when I girth up the saddle. I wonder if the medication he took recovering from his hoof abscess damaged his stomach."

"Could be." The vet smiled like he was having a good time instead of examining a sick horse. "His teeth need to be floated. He has a couple sharp points. The behavior Abby describes at feeding time does point to a mild ulcer. You know the treatment. How do you want to go forward?"

Miss Elena sighed. "I hate to start him on drugs first thing. And the expense of having him scoped is way out of my budget. The barn owner would say get rid of him and get a new lesson horse. If you think it'd be okay, I'd like to try a natural remedy my grandma used. It's slippery elm and other herbs." She rolled her hands like she was mixing the concoction. "Plus a good measure of probiotics with rice bran meal and flax."

"Nothing wrong with starting with a conservative treatment. But if you don't see improvement, we need to make the decision on the more expensive path. And what if we work out a deal for his care? I have a five-year-old niece developing horse fever. Think you could help me out?"

Nodding, Miss Elena smiled.

Abby felt invisible. Did they remember she was there? "Should I put Rio in the pasture?"

She tried not to be obvious about rolling her eyes as she drew Miss Elena's attention from the vet. She didn't recognize the bold new her. But being shy would get her nowhere, and her first riding lesson was today. He still had five horses to go, and he'd better not take up her lesson time doing it.

"Put him in his stall, please. Add hay to his slow-feeder to keep him busy. When we're finished here, I'll show you how to mix up my secret family tummy-gize remedy."

Abby put Rio away and got to work cleaning the stalls. She didn't mind at all. In fact, she was getting better at it, and she liked it. She dipped the fork under the poop pile and shook it side to side to drop out excess bedding. Then she dumped the manure into the wheeled muck cart. The best part was respreading the fluffy shavings, making the stall cozy.

She carried each pair of water buckets to the back of the barn and emptied the leftover water. After a squirt of blue soap, she scrubbed the inside, rinsed, and returned the clean empty buckets to the stall.

The vet seemed to want Miss Elena to show him every animal in the barn, including the cat. Miss Elena would run out of day and not have time for Abby's lesson. Was he never going to leave?

CHAPTER THREE

FIRST LESSON

*W*hen the vet *finally* left, Miss Elena rummaged in the feed room and came out carrying a dishpan full of jugs, bottles, and tins. "Want to help?"

"For sure."

"Great. Then I still have time left in my morning to give you your first lesson."

In her eagerness to help with the tummy-gize, Abby fumbled with the lids. "Freckles? I'm going to get to ride Freckles?" She scooped up a tin box after knocking it off the table. "I met him the night I applied for the job. He's so cute. I thought for sure he had a girl of his own."

"He's a great guy. I'm very fond of him. He's my go-to lesson pony. I wish I had another just like him." Miss Elena took pinches of herbs from a few tins and tossed them into a stainless bowl as if she were a chef. After a thorough stir, she picked up the bowl and headed to Rio's stall. "Open his door for me, please." She watched the horse sniff and sample the mixture. "He seems to like it okay. Go get Freckles."

Abby draped a halter and lead rope over her shoulder, and she couldn't help the skip in her step. *My first lesson!* She caught the gelding easily and soon had him in the crossties by the tack room. "I'm so happy we are going to be friends."

As she ran the soft brush over him with one hand, she stroked his coat with the other in an easy one-two rhythm. "I know you've taught lots of girls to ride, and I can't wait to be the next one. Don't expect too much. I'll do my best, but I don't know anything yet." She picked out a superfine bristle brush for his face. As she flicked dust from his cheeks, he closed his eyes as if he adored being adored.

After brushing his whole body, she gathered his tack and waited for Miss Elena to finish with Rio. "You nervous? 'Cause I'm nervous. Or maybe I'm scared—just a little. Not that you'd hurt me or anything, but I knew a girl once who fell off on her first time riding and broke her collarbone. She didn't want to ride after that."

Abby bit on her lip. "That would make me sad if I got so scared I couldn't ride. Am I talking too much? Sometimes I do that if I get nervous."

When the pony bobbed his head as if saying yes, she laughed and shooed a fly from around his eye.

"You ready for this?" Miss Elena slid the saddle blanket onto the pony's back and smoothed it flat. "Let's see you fit the saddle."

Abby gulped but put one hand on the pommel and one on the cantle. She lifted it from the rack and set it in place on Freckles's short back.

"Rock the saddle from one side to the other and feel it settle into the hollow right behind his shoulders. Lightly girth up. Step back and look at the placement. Is the pad squared to the saddle? Is the girth in a straight line?"

Concentrating like it was a math test, Abby followed the steps. "It's straight."

"So far so good. Now pull the saddle blanket up in the center—here." Miss Elena pointed to the withers. "It's called tenting. The idea is to keep the pressure over the withers to a minimum."

"I did it!"

"On to the bridle. Freckles won't give you any trouble getting it on, but one of these days, I'll teach you how to handle a horse that refuses the bit."

A grin took over Abby's face like she'd just eaten a fudge-covered bowl of vanilla ice cream with rainbow sprinkles on top. Miss Elena was thinking of things to teach her—one of these days. She planned to work at the barn for a long time—maybe forever.

"Grasp the top of the bridle with one hand and hold the

bit in your other. Slide this hand over his head toward his ears all the while moving the bit into position. Stick your thumb into the corner of his mouth, and he will take it from there."

With her first try, she clanked his teeth with the bit. "I'm sorry." She grimaced. The second time, she added more thumb pressure on the bars on his jaw, and the bit slipped in.

"What a good boy!" Abby hugged him around the neck for making it so easy.

"You are almost ready to ride, young lady."

"Almost?"

"Your boots are good. They have a nice-sized heel so your feet won't slip through the stirrups. These stirrup bands are to pop off should that happen. Even so, proper footwear is important. You need a helmet. I have several hanging in the tack room. Slip in one of the disposable linings and twist the knob in the back to fit your head."

Ready to go, Abby led Freckles and followed Miss Elena to the round pen. "Don't let me being nervous make *you* nervous. You know all this, and if you'll teach me everything, I'll bring you apples. How would you like lots of apples? But only if you don't drop me. Deal?"

In the round pen, Miss Elena checked the girth and boosted Abby into the saddle.

Joy welled in Abby. How awesome that this four-legged animal would let her ride him! "This must be what holding a hummingbird feels like. Or swimming with dolphins."

"Or having a butterfly land on you. I get that feeling every time I ride too." Miss Elena checked the tack. "Length of the stirrups looks good." With a push here and a nudge there, she adjusted Abby's posture. "That's better. Stand in the stirrups and let your heels sink deep. For the first few rides, turn your toes out. It will put your leg in a powerful position and help you feel secure." Miss Elena rattled on as she let the lunge line slip through her hands. She encouraged the pony to walk in circles around her.

After several circles, Abby was so focused on Miss Elena's chatter she forgot to be nervous.

"A few things you must know right away—how to go, stop, and turn either way."

Abby listened like her life depended on it. "Go. Stop. Turn." Following the instructor's directions, she tried out her new skills. After Abby demonstrated a clear understanding of how to ask for the movements she wanted, Miss Elena unclipped the pony from the line. She continued to explain more basic horsemanship techniques as Abby practiced each one. Freckles proved himself to be an excellent and patient teacher. He never tried to buck her off no matter how off-balance in the saddle she was.

Soon, Abby could confidently walk the pony around and guide him anywhere she wanted to go. "Why was I nervous? This is amazing. I always knew riding would be amazing, and it's better than that."

"You have gotten off to a terrific start. Think we should quit for the day?"

She turned the pony toward the teacher. "But I was hoping to try a trot. Please, Miss Elena. You haven't ridden until you've trotted. We could wait to canter until next time."

Miss Elena laughed. "Yes, let's wait on the canter. But go ahead and ask him to trot if you feel that confident. Your balance may not be what you think it is, so be prepared to grab mane."

Abby squeezed her legs on the pony's sides, and he walked off. Then she squeezed again, and he walked a bit faster.

"You may need to tap him with your heels. Usually, it takes a crop to energize him. He's not one to waste energy. You have to be serious about trotting, or you will only get a 'maybe later' answer from him."

After another squeeze, Abby pulled her lower legs out wide and slapped them against the pony. He leapt forward into a bouncy trot, throwing her head and shoulders back. She dropped the reins and gripped the pommel. "Found the Go button!" She bounced in the saddle several steps before she said, "Whoa."

If she hadn't braced with her feet and grabbed the front of the saddle, she would've flown over his head at the stop. "Is that your favorite word?" Jazzed by the adventure, she felt light and fun like the bubbles in a soda. "Can I try again, please?"

Miss Elena glanced at her watch. "Just a few more minutes today. See if you can get a smoother transition from walk to trot. Don't make the ask so big of a kick that he jumps into it."

Trying again, Abby squeezed, then tapped her heels on the pony. His trot bounced her in the saddle, and she slipped off-center. On the next bounce, she righted herself only to be tossed the other way. As she slid farther, her foot came out of the stirrup. "Wh—oa," she stuttered. "Wh—oa."

Freckles stopped like he'd come to a cliff.

"He's good at stopping." Laughing, Abby leaned forward and hugged his neck. "And I sure don't need to ask him twice."

"True. If a lesson pony has a special talent, you want it to be whoa." Miss Elena pointed for them to go again. "Follow the trot rhythm with your body this time. It's more of a forward movement than an up and down one."

Abby searched for the lost stirrup with her toe and jammed her heel down. The minute she felt secure, she asked the pony to trot again. She tried to post the rough trot like the other girls but lost her balance slipping way to the side.

As Abby clung to Freckles's neck, Miss Elena caught the rein with one hand and Abby's belt with the other. The trainer slowed the pony as she hoisted Abby back into the saddle.

"I almost got it." Smiling, Abby squared herself in the saddle. "Everyone makes this look so easy, but it's way not. Can I try again?"

"With practice, you will make it look easy too. But not all in one day."

"When can I ride again? School starts in a few weeks, and I really want to be good at riding by then."

"*You* are more determined than most." Laughing again, Miss Elena snorted a laugh and covered her mouth.

Abby laughed along.

"How about Monday afternoon—after the chores are done but before the horses are brought in for the night?"

"Thank you! You'll see. I'm a fast learner, and I'll be able to trot in no time. And gallop! I've always wanted to gallop like they do in the movies."

The trainer squeezed and rubbed her temples. "I'd like to see Freckles gallop." When she looked up again, she smiled. "That's not his style. A sedate walk suits him best. A trot if you must. A canter only if you insist. A gallop is never going to happen."

That night, as Abby drifted off to sleep, she reviewed her lesson. She visualized asking the pony to trot and pictured them doing it smoothly. She smiled as her eyes closed and she thanked God for Freckles.

In the morning, she ached in places she'd never noticed before. "Ouch, ouch." She groaned and stretched, rolling her shoulders forward and back. "Nothing to this riding—you're just sitting on a horse. That's what people say—yeah right." She dug her fingers into the small of her back and massaged. "This must be how Grandma feels."

Abby dragged Mom's big lime-green exercise ball from the top shelf in the hallway closet and blew it up with her bicycle pump.

Mom shrugged and threw up her hand, questioning Abby's new interest in exercise as she lugged the giant ball through the house.

"Working on my riding muscles. I don't know which is more important—that my muscles are strong or that I have good balance—but I'm going for both." She carried the ball into the room she shared with Tara and bounced it on the floor by the bed. Sitting on it, Abby rocked forward and back and squeezed her thighs on it. She closed her eyes, imagined she was riding Freckles, and balanced.

While Freckles was a good pony to learn on, he wasn't the same as a pony of her own. *He's great and all, but if I had my own pony, my life would be perfect. I'd live "happily ever after" like a princess in a fairy tale. I've wished for a horse on every birthday, at every Christmas, and in every bedtime prayer.* "Never going to happen, so I've got to keep my job. And that means keep the owners happy. Somehow."

CHAPTER FOUR

AN ASSIGNMENT

*A*fter school started, Abby still did her barn chores plus homework. She practiced riding and never missed her riding lessons. So, eager to stay in the barn manager's good graces, Abby began showing up before school to help with the morning feeding. She dashed to the barn, tossed hay, then caught the school bus right in front of the barn. She didn't even mind when the boys on the bus called her "horse". She had to make herself so valuable to Miss Elena that it would matter more how hard she tried than how much the owners complained. She would not lose this job.

The more her riding confidence soared the more she begged to jump, so Miss Elena let them trot over poles on the ground.

"I can do this—easy. He floats over them and doesn't even jump. Not even a little. When do I get to do real jumping?"

"How about now?" Grinning, Miss Elena lifted and propped one end of the poles of the last jump on the standard cup holders.

Abby's shoulders sagged, and she frowned at the small X in the middle. "No. A real jump."

"Start low. Perfect your approach, takeoff, and release."

Closing her eyes, she blotted out the picture of the Divas laughing in the other riding ring and sank into her frustration. "Say what?"

"Ride straight down the center. Keep steady rein contact. He needs to know you mean to jump, or he'll take the easy way out." The instructor held imaginary reins as she explained. "Rate his speed to be in position to takeoff at a spot not too far out, or he'll overjump. Not too close, or he'll have to spring over the jump. In the air, release your contact to not punish his mouth."

"That's too complicated."

"That's why you start slow and practice. Now get into two-point position and trot the line."

Sweat trickled from under Abby's helmet and down the side of her face. Another bead dribbled down the back of her neck. As she lined up the pony to trot the line of poles, she concentrated. "I mean to jump it. Don't argue with me, Freckles."

The second she cleared the *X*, she stood in the stirrups and pumped one arm as if she'd completed an Olympic jumping course. "Good boy. You're awesome."

Abby worked hard to master the jumps and begged Miss Elena to move them another notch higher. While she loved Freckles for being so steady, he balked at the bigger jumps. How could she ever learn to *really* jump on slow-motion Freckles? Still, he gave her his best effort, and she loved him for it. She patted the pony before she slid from the saddle.

Abby spotted trouble heading her way before Miss Elena did. The woman who was nice until Abby hadn't properly cleaned the wet spot out of her horse's stall strode to the riding ring.

Miss Elena either ignored the dark look on her face or chose to greet her cheerfully anyway. "Hi, Cora."

"Why was my horse not seen by the vet yesterday? I called the barn and asked one of the girls to write his name on the board. How hard can that be?" She glanced toward the Divas.

"Oh dear. He wasn't on the list. What's going on with him?"

Abby kept her eyes down and stayed behind Miss Elena. Freckles pushed into her and would've shoved her in between the women if Abby hadn't been so quick on her feet.

Cora planted her hands on her hips. "His hind pasterns are puffy. I've put him on pasture rest until the vet could tell me what's going on. Why wasn't he seen?"

Sweat ran from under Abby's helmet down her face.

"I'm terribly sorry. I'll call Tom and arrange for him to

swing by again. Next time you have an issue, please make sure you talk to me directly."

"I expected to split the farm call charge with the others, and I don't want to pay extra for a special trip."

Miss Elena's voice remained calm and soothing. "I'll work it out with him."

After the woman left, Miss Elena turned to face Abby. "You have something to say?"

"It was me." Abby wanted to rattle off a list of excuses, but it didn't seem right. "I'm sorry." She dropped her chin to her chest and stared at the toes of her boots.

"That's a costly mistake, and if the horse had a serious condition, it could have been a deadly mistake as well."

Abby swallowed hard as she looked Miss Elena in the eye hoping for forgiveness. What she saw was frustration.

It took Abby a full two months before she stopped apologizing for not putting the horse on the vet's list. Now she needed to start apologizing for being late.

Abby sprang from her bike, letting it flop against a fence draped with unlit Christmas lights. She'd never noticed them and wondered how long they'd been there—Christmas was still a long while away. Maybe Miss Elena just left them up all year.

Even though it was Saturday, she was showing up late again.

This was the third time she'd been late in a month. Part of her promise to be a good worker meant being on time no matter what. If she didn't hold up her end of the deal, Miss Elena might replace her with someone who wanted the job more—someone who would show up and keep the owners happy. She'd lose her lessons. She'd lose her free ride time. And worse, she'd lose being around the barn horses. But things happen. This morning Dad was out jogging, Mom was asleep, and Abby couldn't just leave the twins' mess in the kitchen. Plus, it might have been faster to walk to the barn than ride her beat-up bike.

"You're late. Is this job putting too much pressure on you?" Miss Elena dumped feed in a bucket, and a bay pony flipped his nose and scattered grain pellets.

"I'm sorry. I can handle it." Abby's finger fidgeted in the hole of the breeches she'd claimed after someone left them in the tack room. "The twins spilled milk all over the table, and then the pedal fell off my bike. I'll get the herd fed and happy." She tightened her ponytail and zipped to feed the next hungry dragon.

"I'll help you." Miss Elena wheeled the feed cart along beside her. At the end of the row, her face lit up like she had a brilliant idea. "I might have a special job for you today. If you're up for it."

Abby's eyes widened as she scooped feed for the last pony.

"I need to ride to a farm on the other side of Canaan and bring back a Welsh mare. She's very well trained, so she would be a safe ride for you and lots of fun. It's four miles if we cut through the woods. I thought I'd ride Rebel and lead the pony home. But the two horses don't know each other, so that's not a great idea." The trainer rolled the feed cart into the storage area, and Abby followed every word. "So I was thinking.… What if you rode with me? You're a good enough rider now to go out on the trail if I'm with you. Freckles and Rebel are buddies. I'll lead Freckles back, and you can ride the new pony home."

Excitement bubbled in Abby. "Oh, wow! That would be amazing."

An adventure *and* a trail ride *and* a new pony to try out!

"Rebel is already saddled. Freckles needs to be tacked up."

"I'm on it." Abby dashed to get Freckles's English saddle and bridle. After adjusting the helmet straps from the last user, she pulled down the stirrup irons. Balancing on a hay bale, she settled lightly into the saddle. She and Freckles had this understanding. She wouldn't mount from the ground and torque his back, and he wouldn't rear and drop her.

Miss Elena smoothed her layered black hair under her designer helmet and unclipped her gray Andalusian from the crossties. "Let's head out. Rebel will love an outing."

The horse tossed his head, complaining about standing still at the mounting block. When she didn't let him canter away, he collected into a mass of energy, begging to be set free to run. Despite Rebel's excitement, Freckles followed like the dependable old school pony that he was. He would take all day to get there if he wanted to.

Miss Elena halted Rebel every ten to fifteen steps, then asked him to either back up, sidepass from one side of the trail to the other, or pivot while backing. Soon the horse was as calm as Freckles.

The thick, chilly air was as quiet as it was still. The only noise was the soul-soothing, dull thud of the horses' hooves on the path. Abby admired the trainer's riding style. Her teacher had the same classic grace of a ballet dancer. Attempting to mimic Miss Elena's proper equitation, Abby flexed her ankles and let her heels sink in the stirrups. She urged Freckles alongside Rebel. "Would you tell me about the new pony, please?"

"She's nine years old and fourteen-two hands high. They've owned her since she was two and had her professionally trained. Her conformation is balanced, and she has a fluid, effortless way of moving."

"What's balanced conformation?"

"That's evaluating the horse's proportions overall."

"Oh. She already sounds expensive."

Miss Elena swished a fly away. "With her breeding and training, she *should* be expensive."

Freckles lagged, and she cued him to trot and keep up with Rebel. "Why didn't you pick the pony up in the trailer?"

The trainer laughed, and her smile lingered. "Ahh. She has some quirks."

"Quirks?"

"Quirks are something that makes an exceptional pony affordable. For one, she is a trailer-loading horror." Miss Elena half-halted her horse. "The lady sold her twice, but when the buyers came to pick her up, she wouldn't leave. Ten strong men couldn't get that hardheaded stinker loaded into a trailer. She lives in a pony palace and knows how to manipulate her royal staff. Really, would you leave?"

"Sounds like she's a little spoiled."

"They absolutely pamper her. When you see her, you'll understand. She thinks she is the queen of hearts."

"So she'll be one of your lesson ponies?" Abby mouthed *please* several times. "I trust Freckles to be good, but I'd love to ride a new pony. Wouldn't it be perfect if she liked to jump? Someday I want a horse of my own. Maybe I could save up and buy her."

"There's a family interested in her. They should be in the upstairs viewing area when we get back."

"Oh." Abby's dream bubble popped. Someone was going to buy her, and that was that. "Figures. She sounds incredible." She patted Freckles. "Guess we are stuck with each other."

When they left the woods, they trotted along the board rail fence to the farm. The mare's dappled palomino coat glistened in the morning sun. Her white princess mane lifted gently in the soft breeze.

Abby gasped in awe, then squealed like she was nine. "She's fairy-tale perfection. Just takes your breath away."

Miss Elena smiled. "I agree with you. The pony of my *dulces sueños* when I was a *niñita*." She slipped in and out of her native Spanish as she tied Rebel and went to greet the owner.

In a daze, Abby slid from Freckles's back. "Wow," she breathed. Her fingers outstretched, daring to touch the mare.

"Are you real? You're so beautiful." Her coat felt luxurious like it had been infused with magic. Hand over hand, Abby stroked the pony's neck. The mane rippled under her fingers like delicate, baby-bird feathers. *I'm totally, completely in love.*

Are you an alicorn? Abby peeked under the mare's forelock. No horn hidden there. She pressed her fingers into the crease behind her shoulder muscles. No wings either. Wings would explain the spell the pony cast over her.

Without interrupting Abby's blissful dreaming, Miss Elena pulled the saddle and bridle from Freckles and settled it on the new pony. Then the trainer held the pony by the bridle. "Up you go."

Still in a trance, Abby eased into the saddle. The golden mare stepped gracefully alongside Rebel and Freckles. Abby and the pony moved as if they'd always been a team. "This is amazing times ten. She is so light and responsive. She reads my mind. Just the slightest pressure on the bit, and she softens. I'm riding a magic cloud."

"I was wondering if she might act barn sour and not want to ride away from her home, but she seems to like having a horse companion."

"She's not tried to turn back even once," Abby said.

After they turned into the woods, Miss Elena extended Rebel's walk stride. When the lead rope grew taut, Freckles grunted his objection to trotting to keep up. "Let me know if the pace is too fast for you, Abby. We need to get there, but we don't have to race."

Abby tightened her calf muscles, and the mare sprang into

a steady posting trot. The mare floated like a dream right out of a fairy tale. "We're good. She is so smooth, I could ride this for three days. Maybe forever."

Way too soon the barn came into view, and her heart plummeted into her boots. Her ride was over. *Whoever gets this pony is the luckiest kid in the whole wide world. Of course, the family will love the mare the minute they see her.* She couldn't hold the leaking dribble of tears. But she brushed them away so the trainer wouldn't be sorry she'd let Abby ride the mare home. Instead, she displayed the best smile she could manage. "Who wouldn't want her? She's amazing."

"She is special, and our job today is to get her a good home. Take her into the arena. I'll check on the family. They should be a good match, so do your best to show her off." Miss Elena disappeared into the barn.

Abby stared at her hands on the reins. "If this family doesn't take you, I'll find a way. Try not to be too dazzling, okay? Maybe throw a buck or two," she whispered as she walked the golden treasure around the arena. "If you'll be naughty today, then we can be together. It'll be our little secret."

The arena sound system crackled. Then Miss Elena tapped the microphone, getting Abby's attention. "Thumbs-up if you can hear me."

She popped her thumb high and strained to see who was in the viewing area. She squinted, but the sun's glare obscured the family. She imagined the excited face of a girl watching her new pony for the first time. *Wish it was my face.*

"Don't forget our deal." She coached the pony. "Maybe

start bucking right after the first jump. Not too big a buck. I'm not that good of a rider yet. But make it convincing enough to get them worried."

The trainer's voice over the loudspeaker broke into Abby's private chat. "Show us what she can do, please."

She eased the pony into a smooth trot, then a posting trot in perfect cadence. She tightened her contact with the bit and applied leg pressure. The pony responded by lengthening her stride into a brilliant extended trot. When the mare transitioned into the smoothest carousel horse canter, Abby just knew she had wings.

"If you're comfortable, pop her over the crossrails."

She guided the pony to the small jump and cleared it with ease. "You were supposed to buck. Are you on my team or what?" She tightened the reins, hoping to coax a sour attitude out of the pony, but the mare didn't even shake her head. "You'll have to try harder to be a bad girl. See that brush jump? None of the ponies like it."

Abby trotted her straight at it. "Veer away. Go to the right, so we both go in the same direction. Don't actually drop me— I'm still learning, you know." She leaned forward in two-point jumping position to make sure the pony was hearing her. "When I turn you around to try again, that's when you should rear away. That should do it."

Four feet from the jump, she grabbed some mane to steady herself. The mare hadn't shown any sign of faltering, so Abby gave her a subtle nudge to run out. But they soared over the brush with flying confidence.

With that, she forgot all about the deception she needed to pull off to keep the mare for herself. They turned to take the line of jumps along the rail. One after another, the pony leapt, tucked her knees against her chest, and arched over the jumps. Maybe they could lift off and fly away together. *Did I hear wings flutter?*

"Thank you, Abby." Miss Elena on the loudspeaker interrupted her moment of wonder. "Beautiful job." She sounded too happy.

Abby's show ring smile fell off as reality swept her. She'd blown her chances of the mare staying at the barn as a lesson pony. *If only you'd bucked or reared or something bad—anything bad. But no. You had to be perfect.*

This was their one and only ride together. Someone else would love the pony of her dreams. With a heavy heart, she slid from the saddle and slogged into the barn.

Miss Elena bounced down the stairs from the viewing area. "You did a terrific job."

"And they loved her and are going to buy her." Abby didn't bother keeping the dejection from her voice.

"Yes, they did. In no small part because you did such an amazing job of showing her. She'll have to pass the vet check though. Hold her right here. The family will be down in a minute. I need to grab something from the office, but I'll be quick."

As Abby blinked back tears, a girl about her age followed her mom down the stairs. Her mom rushed to the golden pony like she couldn't wait to touch it. "Oh, I always wanted a pony just like you." The petite woman rubbed the mare. "And you're Abby?"

"Yes, ma'am."

"I'm June Carter. Elena said you've only been riding a few months. What a wonderful job you did."

"Thank you." Abby looked into the mare's eyes. "But she's the star. She's well trained and willing. You couldn't find a nicer pony anywhere."

"I hope you and Jessica will become friends and spend lots of time riding together. I think riding is a great activity for girls. My times in the barn, when I was your age, are some of my favorite memories."

Abby glanced at Jessica, but the other girl was riveted to her phone. *She's only friends with her phone.*

"Isn't this mare beautiful, Jessica?" Annoyance tightened Mrs. Carter's face but eased as quickly as it appeared.

The girl's fingers tapped on the phone screen.

"Jessica?"

The girl looked up, then returned to texting. "Yes, Mom. She's beautiful."

"Aren't you going to say hi?"

"Sure, why not." She stepped forward. "Hi, pony. I'm Jessica. I'm thirteen, and I'm in middle school. What about you?"

The mare's soft chocolate eyes were alert and attentive. Her lips reached for the phone, flipping it out of the girl's grasp. Jessica scrambled and grappled, but the phone landed hard on the concrete, bouncing from its side onto the screen.

Abby covered her grin as Jessica dove for the phone.

"She cracked the screen on my brand-new iPhone! I saved all summer to buy it."

"Oops," Abby said. *Who needs a fancy phone when they have an amazing pony?*

"Who knew I needed a pony-proof case? Horrible creature."

"Maybe you'd like to trade her for Freckles."

Miss Elena finished her phone call and gave Abby a scolding look.

Guess if I unsell the pony, I'll lose my job. No job. No Freckles or amazing golden pony.

CHAPTER FIVE

PONY TROUBLE

"Finally! Friday!" Abby plopped her backpack onto the kitchen chair and searched the pantry for a snack. Before she could bite into a cookie, the phone rang.

When Abby answered, Miss Elena talked fast. "Wanted to ask if you could come in early today. I've got my hands full here."

Happy to be needed, Abby agreed.

"And I couldn't wait for Jessica to decide, so I've named the new pony."

"What did you name her?"

"Stinker." The barn manager all but spit into the phone.

"What did she do?"

"She's been here long enough to settle in, and I felt she'd be okay to turn out with a couple other mares. I was wrong." A whinny drowned out Miss Elena. Abby grimaced at the tension in the trainer's voice. "She worked those mares back and forth like she was a cutting horse. She wouldn't let them anywhere near the water trough."

Abby put the cookie on the table and bit her lip. "I've never heard of horses fighting over water."

"I know, right? Food, sure. I grabbed a halter and dashed to bring her into the barn. I got there in time to watch her rip the hose out of the water tank. Water spewed like a car wash. The other mares panicked and galloped around with their tails flipped over their backs. That stinker wouldn't let go of the float and jerked on the hose so hard it broke off the pipe underground."

"Oh no! That's awful." Abby moaned as she rocked from one foot to the other. *I'm sure it was an accident.*

"And I have to cancel your riding lesson. The arena is flooded. The stinker is locked in her stall in time-out while I decide what to do with her."

She'd never heard Miss Elena fuss and fume before. "I'll work with her. We can get her a pasture ball or some toys. I'll think of something!"

"I'm so aggravated with her I can't stand it. How can something so beautiful be this full of mischief?"

"You said she had quirks. I'll be there quick."

"Don't remind me. Great. I need you. You can get the

evening chores done, then watch the water fountain with me while I wait for the plumber. If we put colored lights on it, it would look like a fountain in Barcelona."

"Isn't there a way to turn the water off at the well or something?" Abby tapped a finger on her chin.

"I can't turn the faucet. It's stuck. The pasture is already a lake and the riding arena will be a muddy bog for a long time." Miss Elena grumbled as she hung up, "Argh, the water bill."

Hum... if the pony's owner has to pay for a lake full of water, could they decide—no matter how beautiful she is—she isn't worth the trouble? The wind whipped her hair free of its ponytail as Abby raced her bike to the barn.

Miss Elena's office was empty, so Abby hurried to Stinker and patted the mare. "In jail? You didn't mean to do it—did you? Look on the bright side—you created a paradise for tadpoles. I'm warning you, though, don't get in so much trouble Miss Elena makes you leave before I save enough money to buy you from Jessica. And I hate to tell you, but saving enough money is going to take longer than I thought."

She loaded the stall bins with hay, then brought the horses and ponies into the barn. Since they knew which box was theirs, all she had to do was open the stall doors, then let a few of them out of the pasture at a time. Never interested in missing a meal, it didn't take long for each pony to be in front of its feed bucket.

The mud-covered plumber passed Abby working in the feed room. Miss Elena slipped by, and Abby followed her into the office. When Miss Elena dropped into her chair and put her head in her hands, Abby asked, "Was it expensive?"

"Excessive wear and tear is in our contract as the owner's responsibility. "I feel bad giving another bill to Mrs. Carter, but it's not as bad as I expected."

Abby tensed and bit the inside of her cheek. "What's wrong then?"

"I have to spend the evening calling the riders to cancel their lessons for tomorrow. The arena is unusable."

"Why don't you take the classes out for a trail ride instead?" Tickled with her brilliant idea, Abby threw her arms into the air holding her palms up. "That path we rode to bring the mare here was amazing. I'd love that even better than an arena lesson."

"Brilliant." Snapping her fingers, Miss Elena brightened. "Thanks for the idea. You're earning your keep around here."

Abby grinned. *And maybe I'll come up with a way to make the palomino mare mine—somehow.* In the meantime, she had an idea she hoped would be welcomed. "Would it be a good idea for me to ride the palomino on the trail ride tomorrow? You know, to keep her exercised and all so she stays quiet for Jessica."

"I'm sorry, Abby. She belongs to Jessica now. We've not been asked to exercise the mare. Don't make this harder than it needs to be."

Saturday morning, Abby groaned when she looked over the pasture. While most of the water had drained away, the low spots were all muddy ponds. The area by the gate and trough was a soggy mess.

She breezed into the barn, hoping to slip into the feed room before the hungry dragons noticed her and started their uproar. It had never worked—not once. The barn full of ponies whinnied when they spotted her. Heads popped over the stall doors, and each pony nickered, "Me first." Except one. The beautiful palomino.

"Are you a grumpy pony today? Say hello." Abby called to the beauty as she scooped feed and worked her way along the line of stalls. "You know how much trouble you're in after breaking the water pipe, don't you? Hiding out won't help. Telling Miss Elena you're sorry would help."

Her breathing took more effort the longer the pony took to poke her face over the stall door.

When she got to the stall, it was empty.

The feed scoop clattered onto the concrete floor. Abby sprang to open the stall door and hurried through it to the pony's outside paddock. Her heart panicked. "Where are you?" She spun and ran back through the stall and into the alleyway where she smacked into Miss Elena.

"Good morning, Abby." The trainer steadied her. "What's got you moving so fast?"

"The new pony is gone!"

"The feed room locked up?"

"She wasn't in there when I got breakfast for the herd."

"That's the main thing. If she's not in the feed room gorging on feed, she's fine. The service here must not be up to her standards." The barn manager rubbed her eyes. "She can't be far. She was locked in tight at my ten p.m. barn check. She would pick such a blustery cold day to disappear." Miss Elena turned up her collar, snugging it around her neck, and followed Abby outside to hunt for the pony mare. "Let's go find her. You can bet her nose is in trouble."

Abby dashed around the barn, looking behind every building while the north wind blasted her face even as the sun peeked through the clouds. She spotted Miss Elena waving at her to come back. "The hay barn door is open. She's got to be in there." The barn manager's phone buzzed. "I have to take this call. Round up the stinker. Bring her by the office so I can check her. All that hay is not good for pony tummies."

"Yes, ma'am." Abby spun and rushed to the hay barn. She drew a deep, relieved breath. There she was—just like Miss Elena said. The pony stood with rays of filtered sunlight flowing through a wide crack in the wall planks. It sparkled across her back, shooting to the hay-covered floor. Dust particles reflected the light and floated around her like a halo. Once again, Abby looked for wings. The mare's golden dapples glistened as if an artist had arranged every element to reveal an angelic pony. Abby wouldn't have been surprised to see a heavenly crown on her head. "You take my breath away. I'm so thankful for you—even if you aren't mine."

The mare nickered as Abby approached and stroked her soft coat. The pony had obviously been rolling, so Abby tugged on the hay stuck in her tail. She slipped the halter onto the mare's head. "If you keep this up, the name Stinker is going to stick to you like this hay. But you're too amazing to wear a name like that, even though that's what you are. Thank you for not taking all the other ponies along on your adventure."

She buried her fingers in the mare's golden coat. "You better straighten up and ride right because, if Miss Elena throws you out of the barn, you won't have anywhere to live. Your new owner might decide you're too much trouble. I won't be able to save you because our backyard is the size of a closet."

The pony nudged Abby and dragged her to a hay bale.

"Behave." She backed the pushy beauty all the way out of the hay barn. "What would you think about being a trick pony? That would keep you busy and out of trouble. When you're mine, we could go to hospitals together and cheer up sick children."

Abby scratched the mare's withers while the pony twisted her head to the side and flipped her upper lip. "That could be your first trick. But you have to give up being a stinker." She held the halter with both hands and leaned to kiss the pony's nose. "Therapy horses have perfect manners. We can do it."

Abby led the mare to Miss Elena's office. "I found her. Happy in the hay."

"I figured." The barn manager stepped out of the office and ran her hands over the pony. She opened the mare's mouth and pressed on her gums. "Gums are nice and pink. She looks fine. Put her back in the stall, please."

"Yes, ma'am. I'm hoping little smarty pants will show me how she got out."

"She's going to be mad about being left in because I put the mares together into one dry pasture and the geldings together in another. I might put her in with the geldings and see how that works out. Let me think on it. The pasture she flooded is a muddy mess."

Abby winced. "Yeah, I saw it."

"It won't take her long to escape again. Don't let her know you're watching." Miss Elena wagged a finger. "She's that smart."

Abby nodded. "I was thinking I could teach her tricks so she could be a therapy horse."

"I doubt Jessica would like that, and teaching her tricks might make her worse." Miss Elena hit a key on her computer, and the printer rumbled to life in time to mask Abby's comment.

"Jessica won't like that." Abby allowed herself to mimic her words before she focused on the real problem—the escape artist pony. "I'll sneak around to the back to watch the outside paddock."

"I'll watch the front of the stall from my office."

Abby strolled out of the barn, imagining the pony watching her every step. Then she ducked around the corner of the building, crouched low, and peered through the thick shrubs.

The pony stepped out of the stall into her paddock with her

head held high and her dainty curved ears pricked forward. *Making sure the coast is clear, aren't you? You're so regal.*

Her knees ached, and Abby shifted, careful to not make a sound.

The mare bugled a whinny, and a pony in the far pasture answered. Then the mare dropped to her knees by the fence and lay down. Rolling onto her side, she slipped her head, neck, and shoulders under the fence.

That's not very regal. Abby covered her mouth with her hand to suppress the spurt of laughter threatening to reveal her location. As the mare pulled with her front hooves and inched herself under the fence board, Abby raced into the barn. "Miss Elena! You have to see this, or you're not going to believe it."

The barn manager hurried after her, and they both peeked around the corner as the pony heaved to her feet on the fence's other side.

"Stinker," whispered Abby.

"I told you. Stinker is the perfect name for her." Miss Elena scrolled through her phone contacts. "I'm calling my repairman. Glad to know how she got out."

When Mrs. Carter gets the bill, maybe they won't want her anymore. Maybe they will sell her to me cheap. "More clever than a whole herd of horses." Abby couldn't help but grin. "And Stinker's *not* her name."

"More trouble than a whole herd of horses. And Stinker fits her perfectly." Miss Elena muttered as she walked away. "In five years, I've never had a horse crawl under the fence and never needed a lock on the hay barn. Better run—catch her."

Abby grabbed a halter and a treat and raced after the escaped mare. She teased the pony toward her with a Fig Newton cookie. "Gotcha." After securing the halter, she finger combed the pony's mane. "Now what am I going to do with you? I can't put you in the pasture you flooded. Can't put you out with the other mares. Can't put you in the stall you escape from. Am I supposed to just stand here and hold you?" Abby grinned. "I'm okay with that."

The golden mare rested her chin on Abby's shoulder, breathing on her neck. Enjoying the moment, Abby crushed her cheek next to the pony's. "Seems cuddling your face is what you think I should do for you. I don't care what anybody says. You're the best. You're regal like a duchess. Beautiful as an angel and pure gold. Best of all—we're here together. We belong together." She squeezed the pony around the neck. "You need a name that says that about you, and I know the perfect one."

She led the pony and marched to the chalkboard nameplate on her stall. Two fingers smudged away Stinker. "Think Jessica will even notice I've given you a name?" In royal purple chalk, she wrote Golden Glory. Stepping back, she admired her work. "Yup. Perfect. What do you th—?"

Golden Glory licked up the piece of purple chalk, waving her nose as she taste tested it.

"Get that out of your mouth." Abby darted her fingers into the pony's mouth. "That's not good for you. Don't be a stinker. You're going to make yourself sick and get us both in trouble. You'll miss me if you get me fired."

CHAPTER SIX

ESCAPE PONY

*A*bby leaned on a pasture fence rail and rested her chin atop her arms, enjoying Glory. With the pastures dried out, herd life had returned to normal. After a full week of Glory being stabled with a sweet gray mare, a mystery threatened to get her removed from the pasture. Her pasture-mate's tail had gotten shorter, and China's owner, Lily, blamed Glory. Determined to figure out why, Abby kept a close eye on them.

The pastures were freshly mowed and decorated with grazing horses. As if she knew she was being admired, Golden Glory lifted her head. China grazed nearby minding her own business. Then Glory pinned both ears, dropped her head, and charged China. The two ponies cantered around the pasture. At the center of the field, the palomino veered away and went back to grazing. China backed a couple of steps before she resumed grazing, but she kept her eyes riveted on the pasture pest.

Miss Elena joined Abby at the fence. "Over a week, and they don't have the pecking order worked out yet."

"She rushes China and makes her run. China doesn't even think about fighting back, but Glory's not satisfied."

"It's perfectly natural. They have to work out who the lead mare is." Miss Elena rested her hand on Abby's shoulder. "You need to stop calling her Glory. Jessica has named her Starlet."

Abby swallowed hard. Another reminder that the pony she loved wasn't hers.

"Anyway, they better work it out soon because Lily's not happy. She thinks Starlet is biting off China's tail."

"Oh, she told me. I've been watching them for over an hour, and I haven't seen any tail biting." Abby stuck up for the pony. "I don't think it's Glory."

"Starlet."

"Starlet," Abby repeated without conviction.

"For the record, I don't think Starlet is chewing on China's tail either. If it were her mane, then yes. But her tail?" Miss Elena shook her head. "Did you order the tail extension?"

"It's on the way."

"Since it wasn't even your pony, it was so sweet of you to do that for Lily. I hope it gets here before the show this weekend."

I love Glory like she's mine. "Lily was so upset. It seemed the right thing to do."

Miss Elena's phone buzzed. She smiled encouragingly at Abby as she answered the call and strode back to the office.

Minutes later, China's owner stormed toward Abby. Eleven-year-old Lily's thin face blazed an angry red. "See what that nasty pony's done to my sweet China. I'm so mad I could spit!"

Abby took a step backward. "That would make me mad too. If Miss Elena knew what to do, she'd do it."

"She should get that pony out of my pasture. China's tail has gotten shorter every day Glory's been with her. Look how awful it is. How would you feel?"

"Just like you." Abby tapped the hard dirt with the toe of her boot. "Miss Elena didn't know about this quirk."

"She's a quirk, all right. And Miss Elena needs to find somewhere else to put her."

"She wants to give Glory more time to learn to get along, but she may try her in with the geldings. If that doesn't work, she might move her to a stall until another pasture spot opens," she explained, hoping Lily would be understanding. "She would hate being in a stall all the time."

Lily planted her hands on her hips and squared off with Abby. "She has to get out of China's pasture and not chew off her tail. You're lucky she's not chewing the tail off one of the Divas' horses. They would chew you up and spit you out." She spun on her heel and flounced away, leaving Abby feeling bruised.

I just work here.

Abby trudged off to get a halter for Glory. A package delivery truck rolled to a stop in front of the barn, and a dog barked nearby. Abby trotted to meet the driver.

As he handed Abby the package, Lily rushed into the barn and yelled, "Miss Elena! A mean dog is chasing the ponies. Hurry!"

Abby tossed the package by the office door and streaked toward the commotion. She grabbed a training stick, just in case. Lily ran ahead of her.

A small dog with blue mottled spots lay panting in the grass, staring at the ponies. It crouched and crept closer in slow motion. When it charged after Glory, she aimed a double-hoofed kick, but only kicked air. As the dog sprang at China, the mare spun and bolted. The stray dog chased her one way and then another.

"Get away, you awful dog!" Lily screamed as she ran toward the pasture.

When China cut a corner, the dog sprang and latched onto the pony's tail. The determined dog gripped the tail for several strides before it tumbled to the ground. It resumed its pursuit of the panicked pony.

"Oh no! Somebody, do something!" Lily waved her arms and screeched.

Again and again, the dog snatched the tail only to fall away with a mouthful of hair.

Abby climbed the fence and dropped into the pasture.

"You can't go in there. The dog might come after *you*."

Lily's voice of sudden reason stopped Abby where she landed.

Glory charged the dog with teeth bared. Her front hooves flashed to strike. When the dog fled under the fence and disappeared into the brush, Glory stomped and snorted. She pivoted on her hind legs and cantered to the far corner where China stood, still blowing hard. Glory pinned her ears and made China trot to the middle of the field.

Lily joined Abby in the pasture. The girls linked arms and stood together in shock. Finally, Lily broke the quiet. "If you'd told me what just happened—and I hadn't seen it for myself—I wouldn't have believed you."

"Same. I never knew a dog would bite a horse's tail."

"Crazy, but now, I know why China's tail disappeared."

"And wasn't it amazing how Glory tried to help China?"

When the barn manager joined them at the fence, Lily bounced as she explained. "A dog attacked China. Glory tried to get it off her. Then she moved China away from the fence line where the dog was hiding."

"There it is! It's taking off." Abby pointed to the dog as it bounded into the distance.

"Those dogs are bred to herd livestock. It's what they do. I'll call animal control for help." Miss Elena gestured toward the palomino with her phone. "The new owner, Jessica, has named her Starlet. Guess it will be okay if Starlet stays in the pasture then, right?"

Lily swung a punch as if battling alongside the palomino. "She looks like an angel but fights like a gladiator. Without

Glory—I mean, Starlet—the dog could have run China till she dropped."

Abby rolled the name Starlet around in her mind. *Guess that's better than Stinker. Starlet is okay—for now. But I still like Glory better.*

"A package came for you." Abby took Lily by the hand and drew her toward the office.

"I didn't order anything."

Abby grabbed the box she'd tossed aside, slit the tape, and held it out. "China can't show with no tail."

"Oh, wow!" Lily fingered the hair. "You got me a tail extension? I can't believe you'd do this for me."

As the girl's shiny eyes warmed Abby, she stood a little straighter. "It was important, and Miss Elena let me use her Amazon Prime so it would get here on time."

"No way! It wasn't even Glory's fault." Lily hugged Abby. "That's so nice."

"I didn't want you to think she was bad." Abby's voice dipped to an embarrassed whisper. "Even though she's not mine and she's full of quirks, Glory's the best thing that ever happened to me."

Miss Elena slid her phone into her pocket. "Girls. Her name is Starlet."

A splintering board drew all eyes toward the pony mare. The beautiful pony had backed into the fence, pressing on the top board until it snapped. Abby looked to the heavens, but she couldn't help but smile. *Glory's not happy unless she's making trouble. She's awesome—even if she's not mine.*

Miss Elena frowned and blew out a frustrated breath. "Every time I forgive her, she does something else. Why did I bring her here? That stinker needs to go."

Go? Abby's mouth dried out. *She can't go! I love her.*

CHAPTER SEVEN

DO I HAVE TO?

The next Monday, when Abby arrived at the barn after school, it was quiet and empty. A blue ribbon decorated Lily and China's stall. A note hung tacked on the board for her.

Bring in Starlet early and give her a leaf of hay. Jessica Carter is coming right after school for a lesson. Then come find me. I'll be in my apartment.

Thanks,

Elena

Abby hurried to the pasture. Glory raised her head, then trotted toward the gate. "You think it's time for you to eat, don't you?" She haltered and led the mare from the pasture. "You win the grand prize—hay."

She settled the pony in her stall and refilled the bucket with fresh water. She inspected a leaf of hay. After patting it to make sure it wasn't dusty, she stuck her nose into the stems and sniffed before deciding it was good enough to offer a special pony.

Wishing she could stay and listen to the pony chew, Abby gave her one more hug. "Wish me luck. I'm in trouble again. But don't worry. I'll fix it, whatever it is. We have to be together."

She tapped lightly on the apartment door, hoping she wouldn't be heard and she could get back to Glory. But Miss Elena said, "Come in."

"Hi. It's me. You wanted to see me? Did I do something?"

"I wanted to talk to you. Now that Jessica's pony has settled into her new routine, it's time to get Jessica started with riding lessons. I'm hoping she'll come a lot next week during Thanksgiving break. Your family staying in town for the holiday?"

"Yes. If I can, I'll be here every day except the actual turkey day."

"Terrific. I'd like you to help Jessica bond with the pony. Can you do that?"

Her lips trembled as the words dribbled from her mouth. Her thoughts spiked fears of Jessica coming between her and Glory. "Wouldn't Lily be better? She's friendly to everyone. Lily would be a great friend for Jessica."

Miss Elena dropped her chin and narrowed her eyes, looking at Abby over a pair of imaginary glasses. "What did you say?"

"Yes, ma'am. I'd be happy to." Abby's face smiled, but her heart groaned.

"Great. Thank you. Who better than you to help Jessica learn what she needs to know about her new mare? I'm glad you've got this."

"I got this." Abby pulled the door shut behind her. "I'd rather be locked in the tack room with a Diva." The drag on her heart made it impossible to see how helping Jessica could do anything except push Glory farther out of Abby's reach. She loved the palomino pony. And Jessica's mom loved her. That was obvious from the way she pampered the mare and didn't complain about the repair bills. She wasn't too sure Jessica cared, but they weren't exactly friends, so who knew?

Now I have to help her make friends with the pony I love. Then, like it was written in the sky just for her, she figured it out. *Helping Jessica might be the only way to keep Glory at the barn since Miss Elena has about had it with her.*

Abby stared at the newly chalked lettering on the nameboard. The purple letters naming the pony Glory had been brushed away and replaced with teal letters—Starlet. She fingered Starlet's new teal-colored halter and lead rope. If not purple, then teal was exactly the color she'd have chosen for Glory. When the mare sensed Abby coming, she thrust her head over the half door.

"I can't sneak up on you. What makes you think I have

a treat? Oh, because I always do?" The treat practically evaporated from her extended hand. "You know I love you."

Mrs. Carter hurried up the aisle and into a saddling area. She carried a shiny leather English saddle, a teal saddle blanket, and matching leg wraps. Jessica stared at her new iPhone's screen as she followed her mother. The case looked sturdy enough for the pony to step on. Hung over one shoulder was a brand-new safety vest and over the other a dark leather bridle. A white shopping bag dangling from a string outlined the shape of a helmet.

From hours of flipping the pages and drooling over the horse stuff in the Dover catalog, Abby knew how much that fancy saddle and bridle cost. More than one thousand chocolate milkshakes. More than she could ever afford.

Guess I'd better do my job. "Can I help?" Abby rushed to the woman and lifted a box of grooming supplies off the saddle.

"Thank you so much. That was kind of you."

"I'm happy to help." Abby smiled brightly. "Holler if you need me." Then, with a little wave, she got back to cleaning another stall.

After dropping her baggage in a heap, Jessica leaned against the wall, and both her thumbs flew over the phone's screen.

"Jessica! Put that away and get your pony. Your lesson is in thirty minutes, so we don't have much time to adjust her new tack."

Jessica glanced at her mom, then tapped more on her phone before slipping it away. She walked to the stall and opened the door wide. As she held the halter and moved to the pony, Starlet dipped her head and dodged the halter, sidestepping the girl and shoving her way out the stall door.

"Don't just stand there. Go after her." Mrs. Carter scowled, but it barely moved the girl.

When Abby heard the clip-clop of pony hooves trotting down the alleyway, she grabbed a rope and leapt in front of Starlet. "Whoa. You sweet stinker. Where do you think you're going?" She flipped the rope around the mare's neck and led her back to the saddling area.

"Nice catch. You're so good with her." Mrs. Carter warmed Abby with her praise. "Jessica, could you get the halter on now, please?"

Abby held the pony still while Jessica secured the halter and crosstied the mare. She waited for a thank you, but none was offered. That's all she was—the hired help. Abby wandered away again to do her chores, but she stayed where she could still listen in on Starlet's new owner in case she was needed.

Mrs. Carter knew about horses. "Take this brush and flick the dirt from her coat in snappy strokes. Then I'll show you how to pick out her hooves."

"Pick her hooves. Ick. She walks in poop." Jessica rolled her upper lip.

"Really, Jessica. I'm so disappointed with your attitude." Her mom handed her the saddle blanket. Without further instruction, Jessica plopped it onto the mare's back.

"Now the saddle. Position it a bit forward, then set it down *easy*, and rock it back gently to settle it in the hollow right behind her withers. That's good. Now attach the girth on the off side."

"Off side?"

"We typically call the side you mount from the 'near side' and the other the 'off side'," Mrs. Carter explained.

"Just so it's not the fall-off side." Jessica exaggerated a sigh.

"You won't fall. This sweet pony is as gentle as they come, and she won't do anything to hurt you."

"If you say so."

As Abby scooped another pile of muck from a stall, she bunched her upper lip and mimed the ungrateful girl's words. It took all of her self-control not to tell off Jessica. *You don't deserve Glory.*

As much as she wanted to blast the girl, Abby bit her lip.

"Watch your attitude." Mrs. Carter rubbed the miffed expression from her face and clicked into teacher mode. "Go around to the near side, reach under for the girth, and buckle it loosely."

"Loosely? The saddle will slip off for sure."

"Loosely at first, then snug it up a little and check it one more time right before you mount."

"This belt is too big." Jessica threw up her hands and stepped away.

From two stalls away, Abby spoke up. "It's a girth. I can get you one to fit her."

"Oh, would you? You're such a big help." Jessica's mom smiled.

Abby slipped into the tack room and got the best one—well

padded and cut back around the elbows for freedom of movement. She removed the bigger girth and attached the new one.

Jessica tapped her foot like she had somewhere important to go.

Abby pushed the girth under the pony toward Jessica and waited. *Was this girl expecting her to finish tacking up the pony?*

"Get the girth, Jessica." Mrs. Carter clenched her jaw, then turned to Abby. "Thank you."

Miss Elena swept into the barn. "Oh, doesn't she look perfect in teal? You ready for your first lesson?"

"Can't wait."

Miss Elena either didn't notice Jessica's sarcasm or chose to ignore it.

Mrs. Carter bridled the mare and directed her daughter. "Get your vest and helmet."

Abby dragged the water hose to a stall and worked her way down the aisle, filling buckets. As Jessica headed to the riding ring with Glory, Abby's shoulders sagged. *That girl is so lucky, and she doesn't even know it or care. Wish my mom loved ponies.*

Water overflowing onto her foot brought Abby's attention back to her job. "I'll save every dime, and someday, I'll buy Glory from Jessica. Glory will be happy to get rid of her."

She couldn't hear them, but Abby could see the group in the riding ring. Miss Elena gestured and demonstrated proper movement with her body. Standing at the end of the reins as far from the pony as she could get, Jessica slouched. She acted more interested in the arena dirt than the trainer's explanation. Her mother perched near the gate in a folding canvas chair. She was the picture of a happy pony owner—smiling and attentive.

Miss Elena led the way to the mounting block where she checked the girth. She held the pony by one rein and directed Jessica to mount. The girl plopped heavily onto the pony's back and clung to the front of the saddle with both hands.

As the mare's back hollowed, she sidestepped away from the mounting block.

Oh ouch. Poor mare. Abby curled her shoulders and back in sympathy. Miss Elena gripped Jessica's knee to steady her in the saddle. When the pony stood still again, the instructor adjusted the stirrups. "You okay?"

"Unless she tries to drop me again?"

"Next time, sit lightly in the saddle." Miss Elena pointed in the direction Jessica should walk *her* pony. *Her pony.*

Abby shut off the water. *I'm a selfish person. I should be happy for Jessica—she's got the greatest pony ever. I couldn't buy her, and she needed a family.*

Soon Jessica was circling and stopping as capable as other girls. The moment of truth was at hand. Miss Elena would ask the girl if she wanted to trot. Peering from the shadows of the barn, Abby waited for it. Jessica's legs thumped the pony's sides.

Don't kick her—she doesn't like that. The pony's ears flattened, and she stopped.

Miss Elena walked to them, likely explaining how to transition into a trot. Then Jessica tried again with more success. But she soon started bouncing in the saddle and pulling on the reins with each bounce.

She hates that. I've got to help. Drawn to the riding ring, Abby gave the water hose a couple quick wraps and took giant steps toward Glory.

Miss Elena hurried to the pony's head and caught the bridle cheekpiece. She slid the reins through Jessica's clutched hands to give the mare's mouth some slack. "Let's keep her at a walk now," Miss Elena coached. "It may seem like you should pull on her mouth to stop her, but the more you pull back with two reins, the more she will feel the need to escape. Use your seat to ask for a stop. Sit deep and quiet your body. Steady but light rein contact will reinforce your cue to whoa."

Jessica glanced at Miss Elena and nodded that she understood. A few strides later, they started to trot again. Jessica curled forward in the saddle. "Whoa!"

When she tugged her hands backward, tightening her grip on the bit again, Starlet lunged against the pressure and picked up speed. Throwing away the reins, Jessica clutched mane with one hand and clung to the saddle with the other. Her screech sounded like a hawk swooping in for the kill.

Miss Elena yelled instructions, but couldn't get close enough to the pair to catch them. Jessica responded with more screeching.

Abby climbed to the top of the fence. *Oh no. She's scaring Glory.*

As the mare leapt into a strong canter, Abby jumped from the fence into the arena. "Glory!" The pony turned her head toward Abby, then rotated in her direction, throwing Jessica even more off-balance. The mare dropped into a trot and neared Abby, who dove forward grabbing the bridle and Jessica's leg, helping to hold her in the saddle.

"Easy, girl. Whoa now. Steady there." Abby kept the excited mare's nose tucked to her side and her other hand latched firmly onto Jessica's boot.

The girl jerked her leg from Abby's grasp and glared at her. *You're welcome. I was happy to save your life.*

Jessica kicked her feet free of the stirrups. "Awful horse."

Miss Elena strode to them. "Thank you, Abby, for your quick thinking." The trainer took hold of the pony's bridle. She led the mare at a walk and soothed Jessica. "You're doing fine. Every lesson, you'll get more sure of yourself, and soon, you'll be cantering and loving it."

"I don't see it happening."

"I have every confidence that with practice you will grow to love riding." Miss Elena patted her knee. "Why don't you ask her to walk but keep her in a tight circle around me?"

"I'm getting off."

"It would be best if you'd ride for even a few more minutes." Miss Elena tried to console the girl. When Jessica gave a stubborn shake of her head, the trainer relented. "Go ahead and dismount then. I'll hold your pony still."

Mrs. Carter ran the length of the arena. "How scary. Are you okay?"

"Oh, sure. That was fun." Jessica curled her upper lip as she stripped out of her helmet and riding vest.

Wasn't fun for Glory either. Abby scowled at the girl and moved away from Jessica so her mouth wouldn't get her in trouble.

"It takes time to get to know each other." Mrs. Carter wrapped an arm around Jessica's shoulders. "Abby, what did you call to her when she came to you like that?"

"Glory. I named her Glory when she got here. She knows my voice and comes when I call her."

"She's obviously bonded with you, and that's a beautiful name. Don't you think so, Jessica?"

"Whatever."

"Apologize right now. There's no call for that rude tone."

"I'm sorry." Jessica didn't sound sorry.

Miss Elena's patted and soothed the still irritated pony. "Starlet is a nice name too, and the pony will learn her new name. And you'll see—next lesson, you'll do great together."

"Let's take her back to the barn and untack." Mrs. Carter took the reins from Miss Elena and led the way.

"Can I have my phone back?"

If her mother heard Jessica's request, she didn't acknowledge it. With Starlet tied, they took off the bridle and saddle and put them in the tack room.

"I think lessons twice a week would be good. Soon you'll be an expert horse girl. Here—go ahead and put her in the stall," Mrs. Carter encouraged.

With an annoyed sigh, Jessica took the lead rope. This time she blocked the stall door with her body as she turned the mare loose. "I've got your number. Mom thinks you're oh so sweet, but I see your devious side."

"She may be a bit willful, but that's how ponies are." Abby defended Glory's honor.

"Yeah, whatever."

After picking up the discarded vest and helmet, Jessica's mom joined her in front of the stall. "She's just so beautiful!"

As they watched, the pony backed up to her water bucket, lifted her tail, and pooped in the bucket.

Jessica jumped back as water splashed. "Gross. Disgusting!" She checked to see if any had gotten on her.

Abby choked back a snicker. No way could she keep her amusement from showing.

"She's opinionated." Mrs. Carter chuckled.

Miss Elena stepped from the office. "Something going on?" When Jessica pointed to the floating poop, Miss Elena groaned and rubbed her eyes. "She has a few quirks, but she's still a wonderful riding pony."

The phone ringing drew her back into her office.

After the owners left, Abby searched for Miss Elena. "What's going on with that girl? Why is she like that?"

"You've got good instincts." The barn manager rotated her chair to face Abby. "This is between us, okay?"

Abby nodded.

"There is a reason for her attitude. Jessica is a girl with a heavy load. Please be sensitive with how to interact with her. Stay kind, and you can be the friend Jessica needs."

"I'll try."

"I think you sense how important it is. Shall we deal with

a water bucket?" Miss Elena put an arm around Abby, and they walked to Glory's stall.

As Miss Elena unclipped the bucket to remove the contamination, the pony nudged her elbow, threatening to slop the mess everywhere. "You're more trouble than you're worth!"

Abby's eyebrows shot up, and she ran forward to take the bucket. "I'll dump it. She was just upset."

"If she makes a habit of throwing a pony tantrum… Well, let's just say pooping in the bucket doesn't work for me. One more time and that's the last flake of hay she gets around here." Miss Elena pointed a finger of warning as she strode away. "I'll find Jessica a pony she likes better."

Abby sucked in her breath. "Do you hear that, Glory? Be a lady. My mom always tells me that. It means use your best manners. Let me tell you another very important secret. If you like it here and you want to stay, then you better keep Miss Elena happy with you—or else."

CHAPTER EIGHT

GLORY DISAPPEARS

*A*bby biked through the barn's main gate. Why was it open so early?

As she entered the barn, the ponies stomped, snorted, and kicked the walls, demanding breakfast. She froze. *Where are you?* Glory should be hanging her head over the stall door whinnying like she was starved. The fence in her paddock got fixed, so she couldn't have crawled out and run off. She should be in her stall like a good girl. The latch to Glory's stall dangled from the post, and the door hung cracked open! "What's with that?"

As Abby peered into the empty stall, her heart clutched.

"Didn't we just play this game?" The beautiful pony—gone again.

Did Jessica come super early to ride her? Abby raced the length of the barn to check the riding arenas. Could she be sick? "Did Miss Elena take you to the vet? No way. You wouldn't load in a trailer even for me."

Dashing outside, Abby scanned the paddocks. She ran to the hay barn where she'd found Glory the last time she escaped. Her breath came hard and fast as she jiggled and tested the lock. She sprinted for the big pasture. Was the palomino feasting on the new round hay bale? She had to be here somewhere!

Puffing, Abby sprinted back to the barn. Her ponytail flipped from side to side. Miss Elena strolled past with bridles slung over her shoulder. "Good morning, Abby. I've been cleaning bridles. Like new…"

"Where's Glory—I mean, Starlet?"

"What?" Miss Elena tipped her head and frowned. "What do you mean?"

"She's not in her stall. I looked everywhere."

"She has to be here somewhere. She's living up to her nickname and giving me grief." Miss Elena hung the clean bridles on the hooks with a sigh. "If I'd realized she was going to be this much trouble, I never would've brought her here."

"It's not her fault." Abby clenched her fists. "She wouldn't just leave. Someone's taken her. They broke the latch on her stall and stole her. And just her. All the other ponies are here."

Miss Elena spun. "I locked the tack room. Nobody rode her away. You must not have latched her stall last night."

"I double-checked that I latched it. Now it's busted and she's gone." Images of a scared Glory being dragged away to some horrible place made her stomach knot.

"Who would break the latch when they could just open it? Besides, she can't get off the farm. She's behind one of the sheds." The barn manager fussed with a buckle on one of the cleaned leather bridles. "It's not such a big deal. Check the hay barn first. She can't be far."

"The main gate to the farm was open this morning."

"Oh no! That changes everything." Miss Elena's forehead crinkled, and her whole expression changed. "The feed store sent out a late delivery yesterday. He must not have closed the gate, and I got so busy with a new horse I forgot to check."

"Somebody took her." Abby's voice shook. "She knows it's breakfast time. She wouldn't miss eating. She'd be here!"

"You looked everywhere?"

Abby threw her arms wide. "Everywhere! We have to find her."

"Keep looking. I'll notify the police—in case someone calls them about a troublemaking pony. And I'll need to let the Carter family know." The barn manager's voice got louder as she disappeared into her office. "I don't believe someone stole her. And besides, as much trouble as she is, they'd bring her right back."

Abby crumpled onto a hay bale, drawing her knees to her chest and tucking in her chin. "Please come back to me." She clamped her eyelids shut and prayed so hard her fingernails dug into her palms. *Please, God. You know where Glory is. Take care of her and bring her home.*

The barn manager swung out of the office with her truck keys dangling. "I've got a lead. The police picked up a pony they think could be her. It's at the Humane Society."

"How would they have gotten her in a trailer to take her there?"

"If they called the vet to sedate her, it's possible they could drag her into a trailer. The officer who answered the phone wouldn't know a donkey from a pony, so it's anybody's guess."

Miss Elena drew her into a hug. "As big of a pain as she is, I know how much you love her. And I understand how hard it is to love a pony that belongs to someone else. Someday, you'll have your own." She searched Abby's eyes. "We'll find her."

Abby sniffled as she hustled after Miss Elena. "Can I come?"

"Stay here. Finish the chores and keep an eye out. Listen for the phone. I left a message for Jessica, so I expect she'll call. I'll be back quick."

Abby stared after the truck until it turned the corner. After tossing hay to the ponies in the paddocks, she searched the barn for clues. "Where could you be? I have to find you."

Through her tears, Abby noticed the new teal halter and lead rope Jessica bought hanging on the rack where it belonged. But Candy's fancy engraved leather halter was gone.

As anger replaced hurt, she wiped her eyes and reasoned through the pony's disappearance. "That's not her at the

Humane Society. Someone took the best halter and led away the most amazing pony in the barn." Her jaw tightened. "They won't get away with it! I'll see to that!"

She marched the length of the barn. Everything else looked normal. She strode across the grass and squished a fresh poop pile with her toe. "You were here." A few steps farther, she squatted and put her finger into a boot print in the moist flower bed soil right next to a hoofprint. "Proof right here. Find this boot, and I'll find you."

When she looked up, directly in front of her was the forest path. "Of course. If I stole a pony, I'd take it through the woods too." Abby leapt up and dashed to get Freckles. Mounted in no time, she followed the fresh hoofprint trail.

Without his trail buddy, Freckles balked at every sound and log. Abby tapped him with her heels and scolded him. "Go, go. A bunny is braver than you." Her eyes moistened. "We've got to catch up to Glory before she's gone forever."

The hard-packed trail made it difficult to follow the tracks. Then, as if they'd been snatched on the run, blades of grass lay dribbled along the path. "The little grass snatcher was here. Go. Go." She booted Freckles into a trot, but he soon balked and stopped. Abby slid from the saddle. "We are gonna talk about this later."

She dragged him after her. Tiring, she broke off a stick and remounted the cantankerous pony. She asked him nicely to walk on with her heels. He slowed again, and she encouraged him to go. When his balk turned into stubborn, she tapped him with the stick. He lowered and shook his head, but his feet pushed along a tad faster.

On the other side of the forest, the hoofprints dug deeper, like Glory had stretched out in a flying gallop. Confused, Abby shook her head. "What do you think, Freckles? None of the saddles are missing. Would someone gallop Glory away bareback with only a halter?" She urged Freckles forward to keep him from reeling around. "It would have been easier and faster if I'd ridden my broken-down bike." She scolded him. "You're such a pony!"

Just then, a barking dog charged the fence. Freckles dipped his head and spun. As Abby flew into the ditch, the reins ripped from her hands. Departing pony hooves thundered on the ground. With a flip of his tail, Freckles kicked up his heels and cantered away. But he didn't go far before the pony's tummy overruled his plans to race home. He dropped his head in a stand of winter ryegrass.

Without pausing to clean off the dirt, Abby jumped up. She limp-hopped on one foot, then acted nonchalant as she moved closer to Freckles hoping to catch him before he broke the reins. "Oh, that grass looks yummy for your tummy. Did it look too good to pass up? You bad, bad boy." She talked sweetly, disguising her not-so-sweet thoughts.

After she snagged the reins, she dragged Freckles away to follow Glory's hoofprint trail, scolding him the whole way. "You dropped me. Lucky for you, it rained yesterday, and the ground was soft."

Following the hoofprints, she limped up the driveway to

the farm where she'd first met the golden pony. "You went back to your old family? Why would you leave me?"

Dust billowed from the road, and Miss Elena's blue truck turned into the driveway. She jumped out and slammed the truck door. Hands on her hips, she marched toward Abby. "Don't we have rules about riding out by yourself?"

"I know. I'm sorry. I was desperate."

"And not thinking clearly." Miss Elena shook a finger at her. "How did you know to come here?"

"Her first owner called me and said they found her in the barn." Miss Elena lowered her finger. "How did *you* know to come here?"

"I followed her trail." Then Abby spotted Glory crunching hay in her old paddock. Her mouth puckered, and she ran as fast as she could to get to her, dragging Freckles behind. "Naughty girl!" She tied up Freckles and buried her fear in the pony's mane. "You scared me so much. I thought I'd lost you forever."

Her fingers clung to the mare's mane. "How could you do that to me? I thought we were friends."

Turning to Miss Elena, Abby asked, "What about the pony at the Humane Society?"

The barn manager shrugged. "I get that they wouldn't know one color of a horse from another. But, for crying out loud, the horse was a gelding. Shouldn't they be able to figure out it wasn't a mare?"

"That would be funny if I wasn't so scared. There's a halter missing. I thought…"

"I took a leather one to clean." Miss Elena handed Abby a spare halter from the truck.

"There were boot prints in the front flower bed."

"The gardener." She put her hand on Abby's shoulder. "Something tells me you're not going to grow up to be a detective. You're better at following hoofprints than you are at following clues."

Abby haltered the mare then laid her head on Glory, needing to feel her breathe. *Never leave me again.*

Miss Elena tightened the naughty pony's halter a notch. "It seems we've discovered another stinker quirk. She's a highly accomplished escape artist."

"And a homing pigeon, but I'm so glad we found her." Abby hugged the pony mare. "She's so smart. Think what a great trick pony she'd be."

"After the pooping-in-the-bucket episode, I'm more convinced than ever that's a bad idea. And more importantly, Jessica wouldn't want you teaching her tricks. Though if you could teach her to stay where she belongs, I'd be okay with that. Anyway, a new latch for her stall, maybe two, to go with the new fencing."

"See how much trouble you are? But you're so worth it."

Miss Elena started toward her truck. "Oh no. My mind's been so occupied that I just realized we have to get the ponies back to the barn."

"I rode Freckles most of the way by myself. It's not far. I can ride one and lead the other. I can do it." Abby pleaded for Glory's sake. "And I'll talk to Glory all the way home about behaving."

"First off—even though you were lucky enough to have ridden here once without getting hurt it doesn't mean you can try again. And, second—her name is Starlet. I know it hurts, but that's the way it is."

"Yes, ma'am."

Miss Elena's stern look slipped from her face. "Why don't you give me an hour and start back to the barn? I'll drive to the barn and get Rebel. He'd love a good canter. I'll come to meet you on the trail, and we can ride back together."

The truck disappeared, and Abby sat cross-legged in the grass. While she watched the ponies, she picked and shredded blades of grass. "She didn't say which pony I had to ride home." Jumping to her feet, she undid the girth and transferred the pad and saddle to Glory's back. With the saddle and bridle buckles adjusted to fit the golden mare, Abby strapped on her helmet and mounted. "Miss Elena would want us to come meet her by now. Don't you think so, Glory?"

As Abby reached to untie Freckles, Glory snatched wads of hay from his pile. "Packing a picnic lunch, silly girl?"

When they entered the path through the woods, every worry she'd ever had vanished. The easy swing of Glory's walk stride lifted Abby's spirit with joy. This day was all that mattered. "Joy comes in the morning. Or anytime you get to ride." Abby grinned at her adaptation of a quote from her collection.

The soothing rhythmic sounds of their hooves on the hard path harmonized with the musical rhythm of her contented soul. Torn between wanting to shout hallelujah and not making any sound to disturb the perfection, Abby rejoiced in being with Glory.

All too soon, the thunder of hoof beats approached. Miss Elena looked refreshed and elated from her ride. She slowed and pivoted Rebel to lead the way to the barn without commenting on Abby riding Glory instead of Freckles. Both riders stayed quiet on the ride back and engaged with their own experience.

Why am I taking you back to Jessica? She doesn't appreciate you. If you were mine...

CHAPTER NINE

GLORY LOVES JESSICA

A few days later, Abby pushed the muck cart out the back of the barn and dumped the manure into the pile. In the pasture, Jessica tugged the halter over Glory's nose and buckled the strap. Abby wrestled the cart through a rut. Watching another girl with Glory hurt too much. It wasn't that she didn't like the pony she used in lessons because she did. But Freckles was not her heart horse. Only Glory held that place of honor.

Flipping on the light, she surveyed the messy tack room. Her assignment today was to clean it. She dug in, folding and stacking a pile of stable blankets.

In a dark corner, she tackled a cabinet of remedies for every type of horse ailment. A green-streaked bottle told the story of a battle with thrush. Another smeared with dried yellow goop indicated a skirmish among the ponies resulting in bald spots on their hides.

Hooves clip-clopped past the door. She peeked through the crack at the doorframe. Jessica led Glory to the crossties. She handled the pony with ease after coming to ride every day since Thanksgiving break started.

Refocusing on her task, Abby washed the grime from the shelf and repositioned the supplies. A murmur infiltrated her attempts to deny Jessica's existence. Tiptoeing closer to the crack, she held her breath.

"I have to admit, Starlet, you are a movie star horse. I'm still afraid of you, but you seem nice." Jessica rubbed the pony's neck. "Mom keeps saying goofy stuff like 'Nothing better for the inside of a girl than the outside of a horse.' I'm more of a pet bunny kind of girl."

Jessica ran her fingers through the mare's white mane. "My life stinks. My dad got remarried last month." She laid her face on Glory's neck. "He wants me to come for weekends and get to know my new stepsisters. I don't want stepsisters. I want my dad." A sob cracked her voice before she recovered her composure and hugged Glory around the neck. "Thank you for listening."

From behind the door, Abby grimaced. *Ouch. No wonder she acts like she does.* Abby searched the file cabinet in her mind for the right quote. "Always be kind because everybody is going through something." She'd look up the author when she got home.

"I brought you a treat." Jessica dug into a pouch hanging nearby. "Apple-flavored cookies." Glory sucked up the cookie, then cleaned Jessica's hand. As she giggled, the pony licked up her wrist, up her forearm, past her elbow and set to work on the girl's cheek like it was a salt lick.

Abby smiled at Glory's antics until the pony stopped and breathed into Jessica's face. Then the mare rested her muzzle on the girl's shoulder. *You like her. You never did that to me.* Turning her hurt feelings away, Abby busied herself with the shelves.

A minute later, Jessica stepped into the tack room. "I didn't know you were here." She looked from Abby to the pony and back again. "Could you hear me?"

"I work here. The door was closed." Abby straightened the bottles on the last shelf.

"Oh. I've got a lesson with Miss Elena. My dad's coming to watch."

"You'll do great. I can give you some tips if you want."

"Like what?"

"Like be super gentle with her. She can feel a fly land on her hair. She's very sensitive. So when you touch her, do it like you're going to pet a kitten or a bunny. When you saddle her, set the tack on her back like letting air out of a tire. Slow and steady."

"Thanks. I'll try that." Jessica grabbed her bucket of brushes and combs. She kept one eye on Abby and didn't say anything else to the pony. Soon, she returned the brushes.

As Jessica gathered her tack, Mrs. Carter stuck her head in the tack room. "Oh, hi, Abby. Need any help, Jess?"

"I got it. Is Dad here yet?"

"He's on his way, and he's bringing the girls."

It sounded like forced cheerfulness.

"No…" Jessica's painful whispered word wounded Abby's heart.

"He said it would be fun for the girls to hang around the barn and watch you ride."

"Not fun for me." Jessica slipped the saddle pad onto the pony.

Abby back-patted herself when Jessica settled the saddle on Glory as she'd taught her. *Be nice to Glory, and she'll…love you.*

"The girls are part of your life now. I don't like it any more than you do, but it's the way it is." Mrs. Carter fussed with the fit of the bridle and adjusted the browband to avoid rubbing on the mare's ears. "We could cut this bridle path a bit longer. It would look neater."

"I wouldn't cut any more of her mane. I like it the way it is." Jessica stroked the mane.

Abby raised her eyebrows. Where'd Jessica's new attitude toward the pony come from? If Jessica let herself love Glory, the mare would get her through this tough time. But how could Abby let the mare go?

Jessica seemed in charge as she led Starlet toward the schooling ring.

When her dad rushed into the barn, he came with a string

of little bouncy blonde girls. "We're here!" he called. "The girls are so excited to meet the pony."

They gathered around with anticipation-filled bright eyes. Then they reached out to touch the mare. They stroked her face and explored her nostrils with their fingers.

Jessica stood with her arm around Starlet's neck. "Keep your fingers away from her mouth. If she thinks they smell like pancake syrup, she'll eat them."

Other than tilting her head to look down at the smallest sister, Glory kept still.

"Time for my lesson." Jessica cued the pony to walk with her, and the excitement followed. As they waited for the small group lesson in the riding ring to finish, Mrs. Carter checked the girth, then held the pony for Jessica to mount. When Jessica settled into the saddle, she looked toward her dad. He leaned forward with his elbows on his knees in focused conversation with the little girls.

Disappointment doused the sparkle in Jessica's eyes. As the lesson started, Jessica proved she'd learned a lot and was showing promise as a rider. *'Course, anybody can look good on the most amazing golden alicorn in the world.*

Then it happened. As Glory took the first canter stride, she stumbled, throwing Jessica off-balance. The girl flipped to one side, clinging to the mare's neck. The mare stopped hard, and Jessica's grip gave way. Sharply catching her breath, Abby arched her body as if she could help Jessica land on her feet. But the girl face-planted in the arena dirt.

Miss Elena crouched by her side. Jessica rolled to her back

and lay like a confused snow angel. From where she hid in the barn darkness, Abby hurt for Jessica. The little girls seemed to find the whole ordeal hilarious. Jessica sat up and wiped the dust from her face and arms, scowling at her giggling stepsisters.

Later, as Mrs. Carter pulled the tack, Jessica sat on a hay bale, texting. They were both quiet.

Abby stepped forward. "Want me to turn her out, Mrs. Carter?"

Jessica didn't even glance up.

"I got it, thanks." Mrs. Carter led the pony to the pasture.

Abby didn't like the awkward silence, but she struggled with the right thing to say. "I saw what happened. I'm sorry. You were doing great."

"Instead of making my father proud of me, she made me look like a clumsy clown. She ruined everything." Jessica rose from the hay bale and stomped toward the car.

"It wasn't her fault, you know. It was an accident," Abby called after her.

CHAPTER TEN

FOR SALE

The day before Thanksgiving, as Abby leaned her bike on the bushes, Jessica stood in the barn parking lot staring at her phone. Mrs. Carter opened the back of their SUV and deposited the expensive saddle and tossed in a tangle of horse things.

Miss Elena nodded her head in a steady rhythm, listening to Mrs. Carter. *Has Jessica's mother been crying? What's going on?* Jessica perched under the hatchback, engrossed in her own world as she thumb-tapped a message. Mrs. Carter and Miss Elena chatted, then hugged.

Uh-oh. That looks like goodbye. Abby's heart stopped. *What's going to happen to Glory if Jessica gives up on her?*

The trainer watched them drive away before turning to the barn. She focused on the ground as she walked until she noticed Abby. "Hi. Glad you're here. Tomorrow may be Thanksgiving, but I need a little joy right now. Would you plug in the Christmas lights?"

"Sure." Abby turned sideways and slipped through the shrubs. "I'd be okay with them on all year."

"I keep meaning to buy a timer so they come on automatically." Miss Elena sighed. "Always so much to do." As Abby detangled herself from the plants, Miss Elena hugged her. "I'm grateful to have you. You've been a great working student. You're exactly what I needed."

"Thanks. What's going on with Jessica? Why did they take the saddle?" Abby trailed after the trainer and soft-landed in an office chair.

After an even bigger sigh, Miss Elena shrugged, and sad filled her eyes. "Jessica's lesson today went worse than yesterday's. I feel terrible. Even though Jessica was a complete beginner, I thought she and Starlet would be a good match. They were doing so well together until she fell off."

"So she quit?"

"Just like that. A scary fall will undermine your confidence fast. Even worse if it happens in front of your dad and new stepsisters."

"I should have done more to help her. Not that she would

let me." Abby dropped her chin into her hand to hold her guilt. "What's gonna happen to Starlet?"

"She needs a new owner. Jessica and her mother got into a shouting match, and afterward, they told me to sell the pony."

"Sell her! Already? I haven't saved nearly enough." *I can't lose her again. Whoever buys her might move her from here. What can I do?*

"They want me to find her a new home before Christmas. They think she'd make some other girl a perfect Christmas pony. Just not Jessica."

Or me either. When Abby's lips numbed, she realized she needed to breathe.

"Let's get the chores done, shall we?" Miss Elena led the way, and they worked together to fill the hay mangers and then the water buckets.

Abby kept her mind on her job, but the panicked voice in her head put speed in her feet.

Glory needs another owner. It should be me. But I can't afford her. I'm going to lose her again.

Miss Elena brushed dirt off her palms. "Wow, record time. Let's bring the hungry herd in."

Abby's heart weighed heavier as she worked through the evening routine. She opened one gate, allowing a group of ponies to pass. They hurried to the barn and loaded themselves into the proper stalls. She gave Miss Elena a few moments to get the stall doors closed before she released the next batch. With them working together, the process ran efficiently.

At Glory's pasture, the pretty palomino waited at the gate with her eyes focused on Abby. The rest of her herd-mates backed up a respectful distance behind the mare.

"Hi, beautiful. Bad news for you today. Worse news for me." She reached over the gate and worked her fingers into the pony's magic-infused golden coat. "What will happen to us?"

She opened the gate, and Glory walked out, then bucked and bolted the hundred feet to the barn with the herd charging behind her.

"Stinker." Abby shook her head. "And so wonderful. Nobody understands you like I do. I have to find a way to keep us together."

In the feed room, Abby filled the rolling barrel with grain as the noise level in the barn heightened. Nickers echoed, some ponies banged their buckets, and others kicked the sides of the stalls. Then she hurried to each animal and portioned out their evening rations. Soon the only sound in the barn was crunching and lip smacking. Even listening to the ponies eating didn't cheer her up.

She found Miss Elena at her computer, a deep frown tugging the corners of her mouth. Abby shifted to peer over the barn manager's shoulder and swallowed hard. There was no bad picture of Glory, but the one on the screen was one Abby took and absolutely her favorite. The perfect photo showed the mare cantering toward the camera. In the process of shaking her head, her ears flopped, making beautiful also look adorably quirky.

Noticing Abby behind her, Miss Elena sighed. "I can't

use *your* picture to sell her. I just can't. It wouldn't be right." She selected the standard from-the-side pose, showing off her conformation. It took a couple minutes to add the pertinent information to the flyer before the printer in the corner squeaked to life.

"Would you take the flyer with you and ask the manager at the yogurt store to post it for me? The feed store is out of your way, so I'll do that tomorrow when it's quiet here."

Me? Why me? I'm the one who doesn't want her to be sold.

"Yes, ma'am." Abby walked to the printer and pulled off the flyer without looking at it. The thought of the barn without Glory was too painful to consider. Abby shook away the image of her empty stall. Pushing the reality of her assigned errand out of her mind, she willed her feet forward.

The memory of finding the working student position flyer stopped her short at the yogurt shop. *My life changed forever that day.* She unrolled the sale poster for Glory. Then she closed her eyes to block out the vision. But even in her mind, she could still see the one she loved—for sale. She wanted to rip it to shreds.

I can't put this up. Feels like selling something I need to live and breathe. There has to be another way. Abby rolled up the flyer and stuffed it in her bike basket. She jumped onto her bike, but a sky blue paper drew her eye—Hand-Raised Lop-Eared Bunnies For Sale. "Cuteness."

At home, Dad was pulling dinner from the oven as the twins were finishing their homework. "Will Mom and Tara be home for dinner?"

"Mom should walk in the door any minute. But Tara is closing the store tonight, so she'll be late."

Without another word, Abby headed to get cleaned up. When she slogged into her room, the first thing she saw was the poster-sized photo of Glory Miss Elena almost used to sell her. "Not fair. I love you. If you are taken…" Abby put a hand on the photo. "Will I ever be able to go back to the barn? Why would I?"

Her favorite framed quote from Eleanor Roosevelt never failed to reset her mood. "Today is a gift. That's why it's called the present."

Abby slumped. "I'm just not feeling it."

She snatched a canary yellow shirt and comfy stretch pants on her way to the shower. The warm water washed the grime off, but did nothing to help her feel better.

At dinner, the family chatted about their day. Abby couldn't talk about the big event in her day, or she'd be bawling. Then Dad asked, "How's life at the barn? Seems like every time I see you you're on your way there. You enjoying it?"

Abby shoved a bite of casserole into her mouth, hoping to get away with only nodding.

"Making friends?"

"Uh-huh. Lily and Jessica."

"Your mom and I want to come watch you ride sometime and meet your new friends."

"That would be nice," Abby mumbled. Then her spirit whispered, "Tell them." She swallowed. "You know that palomino I'm always talking about? The family who bought her has decided they don't want her. They want her sold before Christmas."

"What did she do?" Mom asked.

"Nothing, really. She gets herself into things sometimes, but she's a terrific riding pony. It was the girl. She's just a beginner. She fell off and got scared. She's mad at her life, and she only wants to scroll on her phone."

"I see."

Abby pulled a deep breath into her chest and spoke bravely. "Do you think we could buy her? I would love her so much. I already do." She wanted to get on her knees and beg. "I could teach the twins to ride too. Our family doesn't have any pets, and a pony would be perfect."

Dad stirred his casserole. "How much is a pony?"

"She's a registered Welsh Mountain Pony. The most beautiful dappled palomino with a white mane and tail. Only seven years old and very well trained. She jumps and can do dressage. She's a bargain because she has a few adorable personality quirks. I named her Glory."

"How much is a pony?"

"She's... she's six thousand five hundred."

"Whoa. That's horse talk for stop, please." Mom dropped her fork. "Not only can we not afford that fancy price tag, but we also can't afford anything that eats and needs a vet."

Abby looked from Mom to Dad. Her face flushed and her heart pounded. With the deep breath came the tears. "But I love her. I'll pay you back if it takes the rest of my life." Her lip puckered, and she gulped when she swallowed.

"I doubt you have any concept of how much money that actually is." Dad laced his fingers and rested his hands on top of his head like he was helping his brain not explode.

From the stunned look still on her mom's face, Abby knew they couldn't help her. She pushed back from the table and ran to her room. Slamming the door didn't feel as good as she thought it might.

After pulling her tin cashbox from under the bed, she opened the ledger she kept with it. She checked the total, then counted the cash, hoping she was bad at math. Except for buying the tail extension for China and Lily, she'd saved every dollar she'd earned at the barn. But the totals matched. "Way short. And it's not going to change, no matter how many times I count it."

There is nothing more I can do. It's over.

The next morning on her way to the barn, Abby stopped at the yogurt shop. With a broken heart, she dutifully surrendered the sale poster to the store manager.

From peeking at the phone log yesterday, Abby knew Miss Elena had gotten calls about Glory. She didn't know and didn't want to know if anyone had come to see her. For the first time since Abby got her working student job, she didn't want to go to the barn.

The Christmas lights on the fence glowed, but they only

made her grumpier. Her stride faltered. *Why is Glory in the crossties?*

Abby's arms slid around the mare's neck. "Someone coming to look at you?"

The pony's thick coat felt soft. Every hair in her mane and tail were detangled perfectly. Her ears, chin hairs, and fetlocks had been trimmed. "You're show ready. You'll make some girl's Christmas dreams come true. And break my heart."

Abby clung to Glory's neck, and her mind raced with ideas to make the pony hers. "If I show you the funniest commercial ever, could you act like the pony in it? A little girl stands on the stairs Christmas morning with her parents and gets so excited when she finds a pony in the living room. But then the pony starts spinning and kicking. Stuff crashes, including the window. The last shot is of the pony running down the street dragging the Christmas tree." Abby smiled. "Doesn't that make you laugh out loud? If you could act like that, nobody would ever take you away."

Tires crunched on the gravel road. Then two little girls burst into the barn with their mother close behind.

"Is that her?"

"Isn't she pretty?"

Both girls maintained a wary six-foot distance from the pony. When Miss Elena popped out of her office, she greeted the family and introduced them to the mare.

Abby didn't want to hear them gushing about how wonderful Glory is. *Yes, the pony is beautiful. Yes, she is silky soft and perfect. Yes, she is every girl's dream come true.*

She got as far away from them as she could and started on her barn chores. As she added hay to the mangers, she tried to get past it. *I can't do anything about Glory, so I can be mad and sad or remember how much I love just being at the barn.*

It wasn't long before Miss Elena led the pony outside to the round pen with the two dark-haired girls skipping beside her. After a few minutes of bickering about who would ride the pony first, they did "Eeny, Meeny, Miny, Moe" to choose.

As Abby moved around in the barn filling hay mangers, she kept one eye on Glory's future. The mare bobbled a step and soldiered on. Then after another circle, she tripped. The young rider squealed and grabbed the saddle.

"My turn," the other sister demanded.

But Miss Elena cued the pony to stop.

"I wasn't done," whined the first sister.

As she ran her hand down the inside of Glory's leg, Miss Elena's face tightened.

Abby cranked off the water and ran to the round pen. "What's wrong?"

"Come to this side. Slide your hand down her leg. Do you feel this warm swelling?"

Abby concentrated as she did what she was told. "Yes. Right here. What is it?"

Miss Elena exhaled a big breath. "Climb off, will you, sweetheart? There is something wrong with the pony's leg."

Miss Elena spoke to the girls' mother. "I'm so sorry. I don't know how I could have missed this when I groomed her today. The vet needs to evaluate her. She's popped a splint on her cannon bone. Usually, a splint is painless, but lameness can indicate a fracture."

Clamping her hands over her ears, Abby shook her head. "She broke her leg?" Her lips trembled. "Horses that break their legs have to be put down."

"Let's get her X-rayed before we panic. Splints are what's left of prehistoric toes, and it's common to develop an issue with them. Generally, with rest and treatment, there is a fast recovery and no long-term effects, but only the vet can tell us for sure."

"How can I not panic? It's Glory we're talking about."

CHAPTER ELEVEN

A BETTER PLAN

*A*bby popped her eyelids open and smacked the alarm. She had to get to the barn before school to take care of Glory. *She may belong to the Carters, but nobody else loves her like me.* She could sleep five minutes longer, except she'd have to put air in the old bike tires. One of these days, they wouldn't air up at all, and then what? She'd be running to the barn. She rolled out of bed, stuffing both feet into the legs of her jeans and directly into her sneakers. She tugged a sweatshirt over her head as she dashed to the bathroom. No time to waste any motion.

She flew down the stairs to the kitchen. A deep-blue bike

with a huge yellow ribbon on the handlebars blocked her path. "Wow."

Holding a cup of coffee, Dad leaned on the doorframe, and Mom wiped her hands on a towel as she came to stand with him.

"Do you like it?"

"It's great, and it's a fantastic color." Abby circled the bike, keeping one hand on it all the way around. "But can we afford it?"

"Your mom got a bonus, and we decided to give you an early Christmas present."

"It's fantastic. Thank you so much." She hugged her parents. "I'm so excited! Look a kickstand that holds the bike up."

"Just the way it should be." Dad pulled a wrench from his back pocket. "So jump on and let's get the seat and handlebars the right heights."

The kickstand flipped smoothly out of the way, and her bubbling delight forced a toothy smile as she tested the fit. "The seat could go higher. The handlebars are good."

Dad adjusted the seat while she took her lunch from Mom and stuffed it in her backpack. "I'll be late again. It takes me longer in the afternoon because I hand walk the pony after school so she gets some exercise and her leafy greens."

"Leafy greens, huh?" Mom grinned as she zipped the backpack. "Isn't this the palomino that belongs to another girl?"

"It's the palomino that is for sale. No matter who owns

her, I want to do everything I can to make sure she recovers and is the best she can be. I love her even if she isn't mine. The vet said the more ice we can keep on Glory's leg the better. Miss Elena has so many horses to take care of, and she says it's helped for me to put the ice leg wrap on her."

"You're a good person, Abby." Dad patted her shoulder. "We're proud of you. We hope the bike makes things easier."

"The bike is amazing! I never expected a new bike. I was going to put new tires on my Christmas list. Thank you so much." Abby beamed a grateful smile. "Can I go now?"

Both her parents laughed. "Yes, by all means, go nurse that pony."

Mom kissed her cheek. "I'm glad you like your bike. Don't get so engaged with the pony that you miss the bus to school."

"Yes, ma'am." Abby walked her new bike to the door, bounced it down two steps, jumped on, and glided along the walkway. "Bye," she called over her shoulder. "Thanks!"

It was such a relief to ride to the barn and not worry about the handlebars twisting when she hit a bump. *What a great bike! Not as great as my own pony, but it's still great.* As she pedaled, she admired the shiny, new, air-filled tires.

At the barn, she parked the bike out of the way and flipped down the kickstand. She stepped away, conditioned not to trust it, and waited. "It works." She dashed to take care of Glory before the school bus came.

She wrapped the ice pack around Glory's leg and secured the straps. "How's that feel? I'm going to take the best care of you, and soon you'll be cantering in the pasture again."

She loved the barn in the early morning hours. The horses all munched hay, and otherwise, only the rafter birds stirred the air. It came to be a time with Glory that Abby treasured. The two of them together made her content with the world.

After school, Abby did her routine backward. She rode the bus to the barn and then her bike home. Glory was not a happy patient. The pony didn't like confinement and was taking it out on the stall walls. If she wasn't kicking it, she was biting the wood.

She'd not seen Jessica since the day they announced the pony was for sale again. It seemed the Carters left taking care of the pony up to Miss Elena, and as far as Abby knew, Jessica hadn't even been in to see her.

Abby shifted in the bus seat every other minute. She balanced on the balls of her feet and released her nerves by jittering her legs. *What would the vet say?* When she arrived, the vet's white truck was parked in the barn alleyway. He put his hand up and stopped Abby at the door. An assistant maneuvered an X-ray tube into position, aiming the centering light at the cannon bone. The vet adjusted the device holding a cassette and stepped clear of the radiation beam.

As they gathered their equipment and loaded it onto the truck, Abby got in the way. "Is Glory going to be all right?"

"Glory? We didn't examine a horse named Glory."

"Starlet. Some people call her Starlet, but her real name is Glory." When the vet looked over her head and smiled, she knew Miss Elena was behind her.

"Abby takes care of Starlet and is quite concerned." Miss Elena slipped her hands onto Abby's shoulders.

"I see. We will send Elena the digital X-rays and then be able to tell you for sure. From palpitating the leg, I think I can safely say she'll make a complete recovery."

"That's the best news ever!" Abby's relief sang out.

"You're already doing cold water therapy, ice, and rest. I have some anti-inflammatory cream on the truck, and I want you to rub it on her leg twice a day."

"I can do that."

Miss Elena leaned around where she could see Abby's face. "Nice of you, but you've already done so much. It's up to Mrs. Carter and Jessica to arrange care for the mare as she heals."

"They don't love her like I do. Even if getting her better means someone else will buy her, I have to help her so her leg doesn't hurt anymore."

The vet moved to leave. "With a nurse as dedicated as you, she'll be good as new in no time at all. If the X-rays indicate otherwise, I'll be more surprised than anyone."

For the next weeks, Abby rode her sparkling new bike to the barn every morning. She admired the colors that shone in the light and the tires that didn't go flat and the handlebars that stayed straight. *My parents can't give me a pony—I get that—but they give me what I need. I'm so lucky.*

Every day, Abby did the ice therapy and checked for heat

and swelling so she could report any changes to Miss Elena. Taking care of Glory made Abby love her more than ever. Just being with the pony was enough. It would have to be. She didn't have to own her, and she didn't have to ride her. If the next person who bought the pony moved her to another barn, it would break her heart, but her life was richer because she'd had Glory in it.

When you can't be with the horse you love, you have to saddle another and canter on. "That's so good. It must be a famous quote. Because if you never saddle another horse, perfection would be the enemy of a wonderful thing."

The day came when Glory could go back to her old pasture with the other mares. Abby dreaded the pony being for sale again, but what could she do? Christmas passed with no palomino pony from the commercial spinning, kicking out her living room window, and dragging the Christmas tree down the road.

So much for dreaming.

Two weeks later, Abby went through the motions of getting her barn chores done, but her mind hung on Glory. Any day now, she'd get to the barn and find Glory gone forever.

She loaded the hay mangers, and her sad deepened with every flake of hay she pitched. Her next toss of hay bounced off the bars and landed in the stall's bedding. She slipped into the stall to get it, and as she stood up, Mrs. Carter walked into the back of the barn leading Glory. Only Abby's eyes moved as they passed. *What's she doing? I didn't think I'd ever see her again. I bet a buyer is coming, so she's getting ready.*

Abby worked in the opposite end of the barn where Mrs. Carter wouldn't see her. *She must blame me for what happened. If I'd done my job better, they wouldn't be getting rid of the best pony ever.*

Not wanting to watch anyone try out the pony, Abby sped through her chores so she could go home. But when the stalls were ready, she had to let the herd in for the night and feed them. Knowing it would upset Glory not to eat with the rest, she had to tell Mrs. Carter it was feeding time.

The woman hummed contentment as she brushed Glory's coat. "Hi, Abby."

"Hi." Abby returned Mrs. Carter's welcoming smile with a cautious one. *Maybe she doesn't blame me.*

"I have to let the herd in now. What do you want to do about Starlet?"

"She should eat with the rest. I wanted to thank you for everything you did to help take care of my sweet girl." Mrs. Carter patted the mare.

"Thank me?"

"I'll put her away, and what if I help you? I can close the stalls as you send in the herd."

"You'd help me? You're not mad at me?"

"No, dear. Of course not. What would make you say such a thing?"

"My job was to help Jessica."

"You're not responsible for Jessica giving up riding."

Abby nodded, letting it sink in. "It would be great if you'd close the stall doors. That makes bringing in the herd go so much faster. I've got a lot of homework, and I should get home early today." She squirmed, just a tad guilty for the fib. *If I'm here, Miss Elena might have me ride Glory for the buyers. I can't...*

"You should go then. Your homework is most important." Mrs. Carter unclipped Glory, slipped her into the stall, and helped Abby with the herd.

After the horses were fed, Mrs. Carter was in the office, so Abby stopped by Glory's stall. "I'll always love you. But be a good girl today and get a good owner, okay? One that will love you the way you deserve. It's the best thing for you." She kissed her fingertips and laid them on Glory's muzzle. "Talk them into keeping you here if you can because, if you go, I'll miss you with all my heart."

Mrs. Carter joined her. "You and Starlet have a special bond, don't you? Elena told me you rode your bike to the barn before school just to nurse the mare's leg."

Abby's mouth puckered as she nodded. "She means the world to me. I'd buy her if I could. I hope whoever buys her keeps her here, though that hurts too."

"You haven't heard? When it came right down to it, I couldn't sell her." Mrs. Carter put up her hands in surrender.

"What? Did Jessica change her mind?" The thoughts in Abby's head jumbled like rocks in a tumbler.

"I can't explain Jessica. Someday she may want to ride, but her heart isn't in it right now." Mrs. Carter slid open the stall door after Starlet finished eating and haltered her.

What could this mean for Glory? Abby hurried to come

alongside them as Mrs. Carter led the mare to the grooming area. The clip-clop of the mare's hooves on the concrete were sweet music to Abby's ears.

"I came out a lot during the day to take care of her while she healed from the splint."

"I didn't know." A giddy feeling seeped into Abby.

"I surprised myself by becoming so attached. Now I can't bear to part with her. I so enjoyed being with her."

"Me too." Abby slapped her hand on her chest.

"I loved riding as a girl and didn't realize how much I missed having a horse in my life." Mrs. Carter rubbed Starlet's neck. "I've decided to keep her and ride her myself. I'm only five two, and she's fourteen-two hands which is plenty sturdy enough for me."

Abby wasn't quite sure why she was happy to hear Mrs. Carter wasn't selling the mare. It didn't change things for her. But she had new hope Glory wouldn't disappear from her life. Things were looking up.

"But I'm concerned I won't have enough time to spend with her because I travel for my job. I'm afraid when I can come to ride, she'll be a wild thing." She rubbed the mare, then clipped the tie ropes to her halter. "Then I'll have to spend my time working her in the round pen instead of getting to enjoy her."

Abby's heart fluttered. "She does need a lot of attention." Could she be what Mrs. Carter needed to be able to keep and enjoy Glory?

"I'm not sure how to make this work."

I can't buy Glory even as much as I want her. I wonder... "What if I help you?"

As soon as the offer left her mouth, Abby wished she could take it back. What had Mom always said about talking without thinking? What had she done? Sharing Glory would feel like the mare was kinda hers. Spending more time with Glory would mean loving her more. Then what would happen if Jessica changed her mind? Mrs. Carter said she might. What would happen if the Carter family moved away or decided to sell Glory? Loving her so much and having her ripped away would be worse than the way things were now.

Mrs. Carter's lips moved from side to side even as she stopped the grooming brush in midstroke. "That's an interesting idea."

"It's probably a bad idea." Abby backed up a step, about to bolt.

"Not at all." Mrs. Carter waved the brush at Abby. "We can work this out. Even if all you had time for was to keep the knots out of her thick tail, it would be a blessing to me."

Still afraid of having her heart shredded, Abby took another step backward and bumped into the wall. Why was she running from loving Glory? Wasn't it better to be with her now, no matter what might happen later? "Eleanor Roosevelt."

"I beg your pardon." Mrs. Carter's face crinkled.

"Sorry. I collect quotes. Eleanor Roosevelt said, 'Today is a gift. That's why it's called the present.' "

"That's a delightful pastime. A collection of wisdom."

Abby nodded as she came to Glory. She slipped her hand

onto her warm neck. "She is a present. I should enjoy her today." She wrapped her arms around the mare's neck. "What if I groom and exercise her at least twice a week? I could ride her in my lessons with Miss Elena. That would keep her weight down and her mind so busy she might get into less trouble. I could keep her tack clean too."

Holding the brush in both hands now, Mrs. Carter leaned across the pony's back and worked through the details of the arrangement. "I pay her barn board plus her veterinarian and farrier expenses. You would be responsible for exercising her and need to be available to hold her when the farrier or vet comes. What do you think?"

"Not another pony here can get into as much trouble as she can."

"She's worth all the extra trouble she puts us through, don't you agree?" Mrs. Carter dropped the brush into the bucket.

"She's totally worth it." Abby needed to verify the arrangement because she couldn't quite believe it was true. "I can ride her anytime?"

"Pretty much. I'd schedule my ride times so you'd know when not to ride her."

Excited, Abby lunged forward and hugged Mrs. Carter. "Isn't life funny sometimes? I thought I could never be happy unless I could buy her, but all I really need is to be with her. How silly would it be to let worrying about losing her keep me from being with her now? All we have is now, anyway."

"Are you twelve or ninety-two? I know plenty of grown-ups who don't get that."

"Thanks for sharing her with me," Abby said.

"Knowing how much you love her makes sharing her with you feel right." Mrs. Carter squeezed Abby back. "Besides, we are indebted to you for the care you gave her."

The mare turned her head and shoved Abby off-balance with her nose. "What? You always have to be the center of attention. Why not? You're the center of my life."

Mrs. Carter patted the mare's neck as Abby hugged the pony's face.

"There is one thing."

"What's that?" Mrs. Carter finger combed the palomino's forelock.

"Would it be okay with Jessica if we call her Glory?" Abby asked.

"That's a question you should ask her. She'll be here tomorrow. She promised to take pictures of the pony for me with her fancy new phone."

"She will? Perfect. I was going to get a surprise for her—if it's okay with you."

"A surprise. How sweet. What is it?"

Abby leaned forward, cupped her hand around Mrs. Carter's ear, and whispered her idea.

Joy painted color on Mrs. Carter's cheeks.

"So it's okay? She'd love it over the moon."

"That's the sweetest, most thoughtful surprise. Jessica will be astonished."

"See you tomorrow. I have a call to make." Abby hurried to the office.

That night, Abby counted out enough cash from her tin box to cover the surprise. She was so excited she could hardly get to sleep. She didn't need the alarm to wake her the next morning. She grabbed a couple of old towels and stuffed them into her bike basket. She pedaled with the breeze behind her, so happy with what she was about to do. When she arrived, she counted out her cash into the hand of an old woman and picked the cutest tiny bundle from a cage on her porch.

Ever so gently, she placed the bundle into her towel-padded basket. With a kiss on its nose, she tucked and covered it with another towel. She kept one hand on the basket as she rode to the barn. Her delight could not be contained, so her face must be glowing.

At the barn, she lifted the towel-wrapped package and talked soothingly to it. Jessica and Mrs. Carter stood just outside the office with Miss Elena. With a smile that reflected her delight, Abby walked to them cuddling the towel. She lifted back the covering and angled the bundle to give Jessica the best view.

"Oh my. That's adorable. Can I hold it? I've never seen anything so darling." Jessica reached for the baby lop-eared bunny.

"You *can* hold it. It's yours."

Jessica was too busy kissing and cooing to the bunny to register what Abby said. "I love it. I've always wanted a bunny, and this one is too cute. Aren't you adorable?" She kissed it. "Can we get a bunny, Mom?"

"Jess. Abby got this bunny—for you."

Jessica cupped the bunny and spun to Abby. "You got it—for me? Why would you do that?"

"Because I know what it's like to need a friend. Your heart wants a bunny. For reasons I don't know, my heart loves your pony." Abby shrugged. "I am so grateful you'll share her with me."

"You're welcome. It will be a big help to Mom."

"I hope we'll be friends."

"Friends." Jessica nuzzled the bunny and smiled.

"Maybe someday, you'll want to ride again, and I'll help you with her. She's a quirk, you know."

"Maybe. And maybe I'll stick with bunnies." Jessica cradled the bunny and walked to the pony's stall. As Abby followed, Jessica rubbed out the name Starlet and handed Abby the chalk. "Her name is Glory. Always has been."

As joy overwhelmed her heart, Abby wrote with a flourish. "Glory!"

THE END

GLOSSARY

- Alicorn—A magical horse with both wings and a horn.
- Andalusian—Breed of horse known as the Pure Spanish Horse.
- Cantle—The back of a saddle.
- Conformation—Refers to the evaluation of a horse's bone structure, muscling, and proportions.
- Crossties—Two ties attached to facing walls or posts. The snaps at the ends of these ties clip to the cheek rings of the halter, holding the horse in place.
- Girth—Piece of equipment attached to the saddle used to keep it in place. May also be called a cinch.
- Half-halt—A specific riding aid used by the rider to rebalance the horse for a change of pace or direction.
- Pommel—The front of a saddle.
- Tail extension—Horsehair that can be braided onto a horse's tail to add volume to the tail, generally used in showing.
- Withers—Prominent ridge located at the base of the neck and between the shoulder blades.

ABBY'S PONY LOVE CARROT TREATS

1 cup shredded carrot
1 cup flour
1 cup oatmeal
¼ cup molasses
1 tsp. salt
2 tsp. vegetable oil

1. Preheat oven to 350 degrees
2. Mix all ingredients
3. Shape into 1-inch balls. Place onto a parchment-paper covered cookie sheet.
4. Bake 20 min. or until golden brown. Let cool.
5. Store in the refrigerator for up to a week or freezer for up to three months.

Feed treats sparingly because of high sugar content.

Don't feed to insulin-resistant equines.

Watch for discoloration that indicates mold. Never feed a horse anything contaminated with mold.

It is best to feed from a bucket instead of hand feeding so your equine doesn't nip you.

Horse Anatomy Diagram

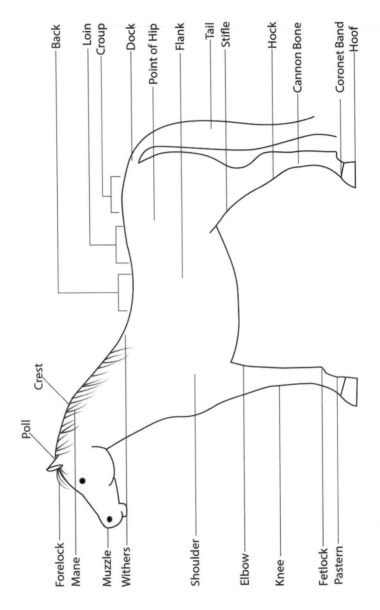

- Poll
- Crest
- Forelock
- Mane
- Muzzle
- Withers
- Shoulder
- Elbow
- Knee
- Fetlock
- Pastern
- Back
- Loin
- Croup
- Dock
- Point of Hip
- Flank
- Tail
- Stifle
- Hock
- Cannon Bone
- Coronet Band
- Hoof

Horse Tack Diagram

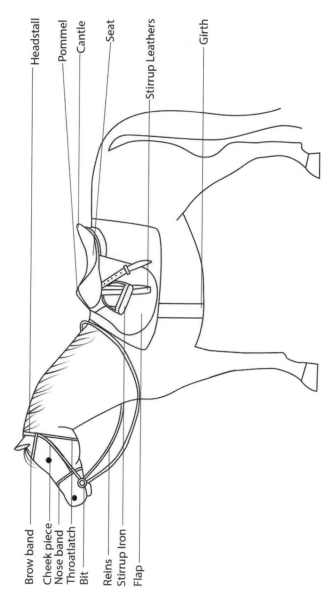

Headstall

Pommel

Cantle

Seat

Stirrup Leathers

Girth

Brow band

Cheek piece

Nose band

Throatlatch

Bit

Reins

Stirrup Iron

Flap

More Books By
Susan Count

DREAM PONY RIDERS SERIES

Abby's Pony Love
When a girl falls in pony-love, she wants it to be forever.

Lily Makes A Way
When Lily's adored pony is injured, it could be the
end of their life together.

Brooke's Win-Win Pony
Eating cupcakes doesn't soothe the soul like hugging a pony.

Wendy's Perfect Pony   Release Pending 2022
She can only choose one—the horse she needs or the
horse that needs her.

Preach It, Grace   Release Pending 2023
A Child's Testimony of Faith
Sharing a pony worked perfectly, until it disappeared.

DREAM HORSE ADVENTURES SERIES

Mary's Song
A girl with grit. A lame foal destined for destruction.

Selah's Sweet Dream
A girl's quest to be an equestrian superstar is hindered
by a horse with attitude.

Selah's Painted Dream
When moving threatens to ruin her perfect life,
an equestrian child star must buckle on her spurs
or give up her dreams and her horse.

Selah's Stolen Dream
One girl's victory is another's tragic defeat.

DEAR READER

Please share your thoughts on this book on the platform you purchased it from to help other readers.

Check my website for any ongoing contests or giveaways. www.susancount.com

E-mail a comment: susancountauthor@yahoo.com
Hearing from readers is a great delight and encourages
me to keep writing.

Please like Susan Count at https://www.facebook.com/susancount where I post only horse-related videos.

I'm also on Instagram: https://www.instagram.com/susancountauthor/

And Pinterest: https://www.pinterest.com/susancount/

Goodreads: https://www.goodreads.com/author/show/14771062.Susan_Count

ABOUT WRITING

Susan Count writes for the joy and entertainment of young readers. She is a best-selling, award-winning author of the *Dream Horse Adventures Series, Dream Pony Riders Series,* and *Texas Boys Adventures.*

She prefers to create stories in a quiet zone. Out her window, her mind wanders through the forest and keeps her in a grateful, contented state of being. She writes at a fabulous antique desk that has secret compartments filled with memories, mysteries, and story ideas. As a member of the Society of Children's Book Writers and Illustrators and American Christian Fiction Writers, Susan takes studying the craft of writing seriously.

Susan confesses to being overly fond of brownies and horseback riding on forest trails. She is a lifelong equestrian and is owned by a Rocky Mountain Horse.

You are invited to saddle up and ride along. www.susancount.com